Longmans'
Simplified English Series

JANE EYRE

I sank down outside the door and wept. (Page 123)

JANE EYRE

BY

CHARLOTTE BRONTË

ABRIDGED AND SIMPLIFIED BY
E. M. ATTWOOD

ILLUSTRATED BY
SUSAN EINZIG

LONGMANS

LONGMANS, GREEN AND CO LTD
48, Grosvenor Street, London W.1.
*Associated companies, branches and representatives
throughout the world*

First published in this series 1949
First Hong Kong impression (10th printing) 1959
Second Hong Kong impression (re-illustrated) 1961
Seventh Hong Kong impression 1964

PRINTED IN HONG KONG
BY THE HONGKONG PRINTING PRESS LTD

LONGMANS' SIMPLIFIED ENGLISH

SERIES

This book has been specially prepared to make enjoyable reading for people to whom English is a second or a foreign language. An English writer never thinks of avoiding unusual words, so that the learner, trying to read the book in its original form, has to turn frequently to the dictionary and so loses much of the pleasure that the book ought to give.

This series is planned for such readers. There are very few words used which are outside the learner's vocabulary.[1] These few extra words are needed for the story and are explained when they first appear. Long sentences and difficult sentence patterns have been simplified. The resulting language is good and useful English, and the simplified book keeps much of the charm and flavour of the original.

At a rather more difficult level there is *The Bridge Series*, which helps the reader to cross the gap between the limited vocabulary and structures of the *Simplified English Series* and full English.

It is the aim of these two series to enable thousands of readers to enjoy without great difficulty some of the best books written in the English language, and in doing so, to equip themselves in the pleasantest possible way, to understand and appreciate any work written in English.

[1] The 2,000 root words of the *General Service List of English Words* of the *Interim Report on Vocabulary Selection*.

INTRODUCTION

CHARLOTTE BRONTË, born 1816, was the daughter of an Irishman who married a Cornish woman and became a priest of the Church of England. He had charge of a church in a wild part of Yorkshire. There were six children. Charlotte's sister Emily (later, author of the novel *Wuthering Heights*) was sent to a school at Cowan's Bridge: this school is described in Chapters 6-11 of *Jane Eyre*. Charlotte went to school at Roehead, and later became a teacher there. Having the idea of starting a school of her own, she went to Brussels to study French: she draws a picture of this part of her life in her novel *Villette*. Her school was a failure. Her father began to go blind; her brother became a drunkard; her sister Emily developed a disease of the lungs. At that time Charlotte wrote *Jane Eyre*—she later wrote *The Professor, Shirley, Villette*. She married Arthur Nicholls (a priest of the Church of England) and died one year later, in 1855.

CONTENTS

CHAPTER 1

GATESHEAD

THERE was no likelihood of taking a walk that day. We had been wandering, indeed, in the leafless garden for an hour in the morning, but since dinner, the cold winter wind had brought with it clouds so dark and rain so heavy that further outdoor exercise was impossible.

I was glad of it. I never liked long walks, especially on cold afternoons. Coming home in the twilight was dreadful to me —with frozen fingers and toes, and a heart saddened by the knowledge of my bodily inferiority to Eliza, John and Georgiana Reed.

Eliza, John and Georgiana were now gathered round their mama in the drawing-room at Gateshead, their home. She lay resting on a couch by the fireside, and with her loved ones near her (for the time neither quarrelling nor crying) looked perfectly happy. She had dismissed me from the group, saying that she regretted to be compelled to keep me at a distance, but that until I tried earnestly to develop a more friendly and attractive nature, she really could not admit me to pleasures intended only for contented, happy little children.

" But what have I done? " I asked.

" Jane, I don't like questions. Children should not speak to their elders in such a way. Sit down somewhere, and until you can speak pleasantly, remain silent."

A small breakfast-room lay next to the drawing-room. I crept in there. It contained a book-case, and I soon took possession of a book, making sure that it should be one full of pictures. I mounted the window-seat, and gathering up my feet, I sat cross-legged. There, having drawn the red curtains, I felt doubly sheltered.

Every picture told a story, mysterious often to my un-developed understanding, yet ever deeply interesting: as interesting as the tales that Bessie the nurse sometimes began on winter evenings, when she chanced to be in a good temper, holding our eager attention with memories of love and adventure taken from old songs and fairy tales.

With the book on my knee, I was happy. I feared nothing but interruption, and that came too soon.

The voice of John Reed called me. Then he paused; he found the room empty.

"Where in the world is she!" he cried. "Lizzy! Georgy! (calling to his sisters) Jane is not here. Tell mama she has run out into the rain!"

"It is well that I drew the curtain," I thought, and I wished with all my heart that he might not discover my hiding-place. Nor would he have found it out for himself, for he was neither sharp-sighted nor intelligent, but Eliza put her head in at the door, and said at once:

"She is in the window-seat, to be sure, John."

I came out immediately, for I trembled at the idea of being dragged out by John.

"What do you want?" I asked.

"Say, 'what do you want, Master Reed?'" was the answer. "I want you to come here." Seating himself in an armchair, he made a sign to me to approach and stand before him.

John Reed was a schoolboy of fourteen years, four years older than I, large and fat for his age, with an unhealthy skin, coarse features and heavy limbs. He ought now to have been at school, but his mama had taken him home for a month or two, 'on account of his delicate health.' His schoolmaster said that his condition was due to greed, but his mother's heart turned from so severe an opinion, and she preferred to believe that he worked too hard and longed for his home.

John had not much affection for his mother and sisters, and a hatred of me. He ill-treated and punished me, not two or three times in the week, nor once or twice in the day, but continually. I had no protection against him. The servants did not like to offend their young master, and Mrs. Reed never appeared to see him strike me or to hear him insult me, though

"I want you to come here," said John Reed.

he did both sometimes in her presence—more frequently, however, behind her back.

By long habit obedient to John, I came up to his chair. He spent some three minutes in putting out his tongue at me. I knew he would soon strike, and while dreading the blow, I reflected on his disgusting and ugly appearance. I wonder if he read the thought in my face, for suddenly, without speaking, he struck sharply and strongly. I staggered and drew back a step from his chair.

" That is for questioning mama," he said, " and for creeping like a thief behind curtains, and for the look you had in your eyes two minutes ago, you rat! "

Accustomed to John Reed's insults, I never had any idea of replying to them. My care was how to receive the blow which would certainly follow.

"What were you doing behind the curtain? " he asked.

"I was reading."

"Show me the book."

I returned to the window and fetched it in silence.

"You have no right to take our books. You are a poor relation, mama says; you have no money; your father left you none. You ought to beg, and not to live here with gentlemen's children like us, and eat the same meals as we do, and wear clothes at our mama's expense. Now, I'll teach you to interfere with my bookshelves, for they *are* mine; all the house is mine, or will be in a few years. Go and stand by the door, out of the way of the looking-glass and the windows."

I did so, not at first realizing his intention, but when I saw him lift and balance the book and stand in the act of aiming it, I started aside with a cry of alarm. Not soon enough, however. The heavy thing was thrown, it hit me, and I fell, striking my head against the door and cutting it. The cut bled, the pain was sharp. My terror gave place to other feelings.

"Wicked and cruel boy! " I said. "You are like a murderer—you are like a slave-driver—you are like the Roman emperors! "

"What! what!" he cried. "Did she say that to me? Did you hear her, Eliza and Georgiana? I'll tell mama! but first——"

He ran straight at me. I felt him grasp my hair and shoulder. He had attacked a dangerous thing: I really thought him a murderer. I felt a drop or two of blood from my head run down my neck, and my sense of suffering for the moment conquered my fear. I fought him madly. I don't very well know what I did with my hands, but he called me "Rat! Rat!" and wept aloud. Aid was near him: his sisters had run for Mrs. Reed, who had gone upstairs. Now she came upon the scene, followed by Bessie and the maid Abbot. We were separated. I heard the words:

"Oh, dear! What a fury to fly at Master John like that!"

"Did ever anybody see such rage!"

Then Mrs. Reed commanded:

"Take her away to the red room, and lock her in there."

Four hands were immediately laid upon me, and I was carried upstairs.

CHAPTER 2

THE RED ROOM

I RESISTED all the way—a new thing for me, and a circumstance that greatly strengthened the bad opinion that Bessie and Miss Abbot tended to hold of me.

"Hold her arms, Miss Abbot: she's like a mad cat."

"For shame! for shame!" cried the lady's maid. "What shocking conduct, Miss Eyre, to strike a young gentleman, your guardian's son!—your young master!"

"Master! How is he my master? Am I a servant?"

"No, you are less than a servant, for you do nothing to support yourself. There, sit down, and think over your wickedness."

They had got me by this time into the room named by Mrs.

Reed, and had pushed me on to a chair. I tried to rise from it like a spring. Their two pairs of hands arrested me instantly.

"If you don't sit still, you must be tied down," said Bessie. "Miss Abbot, lend me your belt; she would break mine at once."

"Don't do that," I cried. "I will not stir."

"Take care that you don't," said Bessie, and when she had made sure that I was really growing quieter, she loosened her hold of me. She and Miss Abbot stood with folded arms, looking darkly and doubtfully at my face.

"She never did this before," said Bessie at last, turning to the lady's maid.

"But it was always in her," was the reply. "I've often told missis[1] my opinion about the child, and missis agreed with me. She's a deceitful little thing."

Bessie did not answer; but before long, addressing me, she said:

"You ought to know, miss, that you should be grateful to Mrs. Reed. She supports you. If she were to send you away, who would look after you?"

I had nothing to say to these words: they were not new to me. I had heard many suggestions of the same kind before, very painful and humiliating,[2] but only half understood. Miss Abbot joined in:

"And you ought not to think yourself equal to the two Miss Reeds and Master Reed, because missis kindly allows you to be brought up with them. They will have a great deal of money, and you will have none. It is your duty to be humble, and to try to make yourself agreeable to them."

"What we tell you is for your good," added Bessie, in a milder voice; "you should try to be useful and pleasant, then, perhaps, you will have a home here; but if you become passionate[3] and rude, missis will send you away, I am sure."

"Besides," said Miss Abbot, "God will punish you: He

[1] missis = a servant's way of referring to her mistress.
[2] humiliating = lowering the pride of. Making ashamed.
[3] passionate = adj. from passion, a strong emotion, especially of anger or love.

might strike you dead in the midst of your fury. Come, Bessie, we will leave her. Say your prayers, Miss Eyre, for if you are not sorry for your evil deeds, something bad might come down the chimney and take you away."

They went, shutting the door, and locking it behind them.

The red room was a square room, furnished in dark wood, with a heavy red carpet, and curtains always drawn across. This room was cold, because it rarely had a fire; silent, because it was far from the nursery[1] and kitchen; solemn, because it was seldom entered. It was here that Mr. Reed had died nine years before.

I was not quite sure whether they had locked the door, and when I dared move, I got up and went to see. Alas![2] yes: no prison was ever more firmly fastened.

My head still ached and bled from the blow and fall I had received. No one had blamed John for striking me without cause. "Unjust! unjust!" I thought. I began to plan some escape, such as running away, or never eating or drinking any more, and letting myself die.

Daylight began to leave the red room: it was past four o'clock, and the cloudy afternoon was followed by a gloomy twilight. I heard the rain still beating continuously on the staircase window, and the wind moaning in the trees behind the house. I grew by degrees cold as a stone, and then my courage sank. All said that I was wicked, and perhaps I might be so.

My thoughts turned to my uncle. I could not remember him, but I knew that he was my mother's brother, that he had taken me as a parentless child to his house, and that before he died he had received a promise from Mrs. Reed that she would look after me as one of her own children.

A strange idea entered my mind. I never doubted that if Mr. Reed had been alive he would have treated me kindly, and now, as I sat in the growing darkness, I began to remember stories of dead men, troubled in their graves by disregard of

---

[1] nursery = a room for children and their nurse.
[2] alas! = an exclamation of despair.

their last wishes, revisiting the earth. Perhaps Mr. Reed's spirit might rise before me. The idea, instead of comforting me, filled me with terror. At this moment a ray of light shone on the wall. My heart beat fast, my head grew hot; a sound filled my ears, which seemed like the rushing of wings. I ran in despair to the door and shook the lock. Steps came hurrying along the outer passage; the key turned and Bessie and Abbot entered.

"Miss Eyre, are you ill?" said Bessie.

"What a dreadful noise! It went right through me!" exclaimed Abbot.

"Take me out! Let me go into the nursery!" was my cry.

"What for? Are you hurt? Have you seen something?" Bessie demanded again.

"Oh, I saw a light, and I thought a ghost had come." I had now got hold of Bessie's hand, and she did not take it from me.

"She has screamed out on purpose," declared Abbot in disgust. "And what a scream! If she had been in great pain one would have excused it, but she only wanted to bring us all here. I know her naughty tricks."

".What is all this?" demanded another voice sharply, and Mrs. Reed came along the passage. "Abbot and Bessie, I believe I gave orders that Jane Eyre should be left in the red room till I came to her myself."

"Miss Jane screamed so loud, ma'am,[1]" replied Bessie.

"Let her go," was the only answer. "Loose Bessie's hand, child, you cannot succeed in getting out by these means. I hate tricks, especially in children. It is my duty to show you that they will not succeed. You will now stay here an hour longer, and it is only on condition of perfect obedience and quiet that I shall let you out then."

"Oh, aunt! have pity! Forgive me! I cannot bear it! Let me be punished in some other way!"

"Silence! This violence is most disgusting." She did not believe me: she thought that I was pretending.

Bessie and Abbot having gone away, Mrs. Reed, impatient

---

[1] ma'am = a shortened form of madam.

of my wild cries, roughly pushed me back and locked me in, without further speech. I heard her depart, and soon after she had gone, my head began to swim, and I fell unconscious.

CHAPTER 3

ILLNESS

THE next thing I remember is waking up with a feeling as if I had had a frightful dream, and seeing before me a terrible hot red light, crossed with thick black bars. I heard voices, too, speaking with a hollow sound. Uncertainty and terror confused my senses. I then became aware that someone was lifting me up more gently than I had ever been raised before. I rested my head against something, and felt comfortable.

In five minutes the cloud of confusion melted. I knew quite well that I was in my own bed, and that the red light came from the nursery fire. It was night. A candle burned on the table. Bessie stood at the foot of the bed, and a gentleman sat in a chair near me.

I felt an inexpressible relief when I knew that there was a stranger in the room, an individual not belonging to Gateshead. Turning from Bessie I examined the face of the visitor. I knew him. It was Mr. Lloyd, a shopkeeper who sold medicines, and who was sometimes called in by Mrs. Reed when one of the servants was ill. For herself and the children she employed a qualified doctor.

" Well, who am I? " he asked.

I pronounced his name, offering him my hand at the same time. He took it, smiling and saying, " You will be better soon." He then addressed Bessie, warning her to be very careful that I was not disturbed during the night. Having given some further instructions, he departed, saying that he would call again the next day.

" Do you feel as if you could sleep, miss? " asked Bessie, rather softly.

I scarcely dared answer her, for I feared that her next reply
might be rough.

"I will try."

"Would you like to drink, or could you eat anything?"

"No, thank you, Bessie."

"Then I think I will go to bed, but you may call me if you
want anything in the night."

Bessie went into the housemaid's room, which was near.
I heard her say:

"Sarah, come and sleep with me in the nursery. I daren't
be alone with that poor child to-night: she might die. It's
strange that she should have fainted so. I wonder if she saw
anything. Missis was rather too hard on her."

Sarah came back with her, and they both soon fell asleep.
For me, however, it was a night of wakefulness.

Next day, by twelve o'clock, I was up and dressed, and sat
in a rug by the nursery fire. I felt weak in body, but my worst
trouble was an indescribable misery of mind. Yet, I thought,
I ought to have been happy, for all the Reeds had gone out
in the carriage, Abbot was sewing in another room, and Bessie,
as she moved about the nursery at her work, spoke to me every
now and then with unusual kindness. Then, too, a cake had
come up from the kitchen, on a certain brightly painted plate,
which I had long loved, but been forbidden to touch. This
precious dish was placed on my knee, and I was invited to
eat. Vain favour! I had no appetite. Bessie asked if I would
have a book, and I begged her to fetch *Gulliver's Travels* from
the library. I had read this book again and again with delight,
yet when it was now placed in my hands, the pictures that
had so often given me pleasure, the giants and the tiny men,
filled my mind with fear. I closed the book.

Bessie had now finished tidying, and began to sew. Meanwhile she sang. She had a sweet voice, but the song was a
sad one. about an orphan[1] child.

"Come, Miss Jane, don't cry," said Bessie, as it ended. She
might as well have said to the fire, "Don't burn!"

[1] orphan = a child whose father and mother are dead.

Shortly after, Mr. Lloyd came again.

"What, up already!" he said, as he entered the nursery. "Well, nurse, how is she?"

Bessie answered that I was doing very well.

"Then she ought to look more cheerful. Come here, Miss Jane. You have been crying: can you tell me what about? Have you any pain?"

"No, sir."

"Oh! I suppose she is crying because she could not go out in the carriage with missis," said Bessie.

I answered immediately, "I never cried for such a thing in my life! I hate going out in the carriage. I cry because I am miserable."

"Nonsense, miss!" said Bessie.

Mr. Lloyd appeared a little puzzled. He fixed his eyes on me very steadily. Having observed me for some time, he said:

"What made you ill yesterday?"

"She had a fall," said Bessie, again entering the conversation.

"Fall! why, that is like a baby! Can't she manage to walk at her age?"

"I was knocked down," was my explanation, drawn from me by my wounded pride, "but that did not make me ill."

At that moment a loud bell rang. It was the servants' dinner.

"That's for you, nurse," said Mr. Lloyd, "you can go down."

Bessie would rather have stayed, but she was obliged to go, because punctuality at meals was strictly enforced at Gateshead.

"The fall did not make you ill; what did, then?" continued Mr. Lloyd when Bessie had gone.

"I was shut up in a room where there is a ghost."

I saw Mr. Lloyd smile and frown at the same time.

"Ghost! What, you are a baby after all! You are afraid of ghosts?"

"Of Mr. Reed's ghost I am: he died in that room. It was cruel to shut me up alone without a candle."

" And is it that which makes you so miserable? "

" I am unhappy, for other reasons."

" What other reasons? Can you tell me some of them? "

How much I wished to reply fully to this question! Children can feel, but they cannot explain their feelings.

" For one thing, I have no father or mother, brothers or sisters."

" But you have a kind aunt and cousins."

" But John Reed knocked me down, and my aunt shut me up in the red room."

Mr. Lloyd paused, looking thoughtful.

" Don't you think Gateshead is a very beautiful place? " he asked. " Aren't you very lucky to be able to live here? "

" It is not my house, sir; and Abbot says I have less right here than a servant."

" But you wouldn't wish to leave such a splendid place? "

" If I had anywhere else to go, I should be glad to leave it."

" Have you any other relations belonging to your father? "

" I don't know: I asked Aunt Reed once, and she said that possibly I might have some poor, low relations called Eyre, but she knew nothing of them."

" Would you like to go to school? "

I reflected. I scarcely knew what school was. John Reed hated his school, and spoke insultingly of his master, but John Reed's opinions were not mine. Bessie's accounts of school discipline, gathered from the young ladies of a family where she lived before coming to Gateshead, were somewhat alarming, but her details of certain accomplishments learnt by these young ladies were attractive. She boasted of beautiful paintings of scenery and flowers that they did, of songs they could sing, and music they could play, of French books that they could translate, till my spirit was stirred to rivalry. Besides, school would be a complete change, an entry into a new life.

" I should indeed like to go to school," I said at last.

" Well, who knows what may happen? " said Mr. Lloyd, getting up, and as Bessie returned at that moment, he said to her, " Is your mistress back yet?   I should like to speak to her before I go."

That night, when Bessie and Abbot sat sewing in the nursery, supposing me to be asleep, I learnt from their conversation that Mr. Lloyd had persuaded Mrs. Reed to send me to school. On the same occasion I heard for the first time, from Abbot's information to Bessie, that my father had been a poor clergyman;[1] that my mother had married him against the wishes of her friends; that my grandfather had been so annoyed at her disobedience that he had disinherited[2] her; that after a year of marriage my father caught a fever while visiting the poor; that my mother caught the disease from him, and that both died soon after.

CHAPTER 4

MR. BROCKLEHURST

IT was the fifteenth of January, about nine o'clock in the morning. Bessie had gone down to breakfast, and my cousins had not yet been summoned to their mama. Eliza was putting on her hat and coat to go and feed her hens, an occupation of which she was fond, for she sold the eggs to the housekeeper at a good profit. Georgiana was putting artificial flowers in her hair. I was making my bed, for Bessie frequently employed me as a sort of assistant nurserymaid.

From the nursery window the main gates were visible, and at this moment they were thrown open, and a carriage rolled through. It stopped in front of the house, the door-bell rang loudly, and the newcomer was admitted. Bessie came running upstairs.

" Miss Jane, what are you doing?   Have you washed your face and hands this morning? "

[1] clergyman = a priest of the Christian religion.
[2] disinherit = to alter a will so as to leave a person nothing (from inherit, to be left a person's property in his will).

She brushed my hair hurriedly, and told me to go down at
once, as I was wanted in the breakfast-room.

I descended slowly. For a long time, I had never been called
to Mrs. Reed's presence. Fearful and trembling, I stood before
the door of the breakfast-room. What a miserable little cow-
ard had fear, the result of unjust punishment, made me!

"Who could want me?" I wondered. "Whom shall I see
besides Aunt Reed in the room? . . . a man or a woman?"

I turned the handle, opened the door, and passing through
looked up at . . . a black pillar! Such at least the shape
standing upright on the rug appeared to me, at first sight.

Mrs. Reed occupied her usual seat by the fire. She made
a sign to me to approach, saying to the stranger:

"This is the little girl about whom I applied to you."

He (for it was a man) turned his head slowly, and having
examined me, said solemnly and in a deep voice:

"She is small; what is her age?"

"Ten years."

"So much?" he said in surprise. Presently he addressed
me:

"Your name, little girl?"

"Jane Eyre, sir."

"Well, Jane Eyre, and are you a good child?"

I was silent. Mrs. Reed answered for me by a shake of the
head.

"There is no sight so sad as a naughty child," he continued.
"God will punish the wicked. Do you say your prayers night
and morning?"

"Yes, sir."

Mrs. Reed then entered the conversation.

"Mr. Brocklehurst, I believe I informed you in the letter
that I wrote to you three weeks ago, that this little girl has
not quite the character she ought to have. Should you admit
her to Lowood School, I should be glad if the teachers would
keep a strict eye on her, and above all, guard against her
worst fault, a tendency to deceit."

I had good reason to dread Mrs. Reed, for it was her nature

to wound me cruelly. This accusation, made before a stranger, cut me to the heart. I saw that she was doing her best to spoil for me the new life from which I hoped so much.

"Deceit, indeed, is a sad fault in a child," said Mr. Brocklehurst. "She shall be watched, Mrs. Reed. I will speak to Miss Temple and the teachers."

"I wish her to be brought up in a manner suited to her future," continued my aunt, "to be made useful, to be kept humble. As for the holidays, she will, with your permission, spend them always at Lowood."

"Your decisions are wise, madam. Little girl, here is a book. Read especially the part containing an account of the sudden death of Martha, a naughty child who told lies."

Shortly after, he departed, and Mrs. Reed and I were left alone. Some minutes passed in silence. She was sewing, I was watching her. A passion of anger stirred within me.

Mrs. Reed looked up, her eye settled on mine, and her fingers ceased their movements.

"Go out of the room. Return to the nursery," was her command.

I got up, and went to the door. I came back again across the room close up to her.

I must speak, but what strength had I to strike back at this enemy of mine? I gathered all my energies and attacked in this sentence:

"I am not deceitful: if I were, I should say I loved you; but I declare I do not love you: I dislike you the worst of anybody in the world except John Reed: and this book about the liar, you may give to your girl Georgiana, for it is she who tells lies, not I."

Mrs. Reed's hands still lay motionless on her work, and her cold eye remained fixed on mine.

"What more have you to say?" she asked, rather in the tone in which a person might address someone of the same age than that used to a child.

Shaking from head to foot, trembling with uncontrollable excitement, I went on:

"I am glad you are no relation of mine. I will never call you aunt again as long as I live. If anyone asks me how I liked you, and how you treated me, I will say that you have no pity, and that you treated me with miserable cruelty."

"How dare you say that, Jane Eyre!"

"How dare I, Mrs. Reed? Because it is the truth. You think I have no feelings, and can do without one bit of love and kindness. I shall remember how you pushed me back into the red room, though I was terrified, and begged you for mercy. And that punishment you made me suffer because your wicked boy struck me—knocked me down for nothing. People think you are a good woman, but you are bad, hard-hearted!"

Before I had finished this reply, my soul began to feel the strangest sense of freedom. It was not without cause. Mrs. Reed looked frightened; her work had slipped from her knee; she was even twisting her face as if she would cry.

"Jane, you are mistaken: what is the matter with you? Why do you tremble so violently? Would you like to drink some water?"

"No, Mrs. Reed."

"Is there anything else you wish for, Jane? I assure you, I desire to be your friend."

"Not you. You told Mr. Brocklehurst I had a bad character, and I'll let everybody at Lowood know what you are, and what you have done."

"Jane, you don't understand these things; children must be corrected for their faults."

"Deceit is not my fault!"

"But you must admit that you are passionate. Now return to the nursery, my dear—and lie down a little."

"I am not your dear. Send me to school soon, Mrs. Reed, for I hate to live here."

"I will indeed send her to school soon," murmured Mrs. Reed to herself, and gathering up her work, she suddenly left the room.

CHAPTER 5

JOURNEY BY COACH

FIVE O'CLOCK had hardly struck on the morning of the nineteenth of January, when Bessie brought a candle into my little room and found me already up and nearly dressed. I was to leave Gateshead that day by a coach that passed the house at six o'clock. Bessie had lit a fire in the nursery, where she now began to get my breakfast. Few children can eat when excited at the thought of a journey. I could not. Bessie, having urged me in vain to take a few spoonfuls of the boiled milk and bread she had prepared for me, wrapped up some cake in paper and put it in my bag, then she helped me to put on my coat and hat, and we left the nursery.

As we passed Mrs. Reed's bedroom, Bessie said:

" Will you go in and say good-bye to missis? "

" No, Bessie, she came to my bed last night when you had gone down to supper, and said I need not disturb her in the morning, or my cousins either; and she told me to remember that she had always been my best friend."

" What did you say, miss? "

" Nothing: I covered my face with the sheet, and turned from her to the wall."

" That was wrong, Miss Jane."

" Good-bye to Gateshead! " I cried, as we passed through the hall and went out at the front door.

It was very dark, and Bessie carried a lamp. The winter morning was damp and cold as I hastened to the gate. My trunk, which had been carried there the night before, stood ready. It was only a few minutes to six, and shortly after, the distant roll of wheels announced that the coach was coming. There it was, with its four horses and its top loaded with passengers. The coachman and the guard loudly urged haste, my trunk was lifted up, and I was taken from Bessie's neck, on which I hung with kisses.

"Be sure and take good care of her," she cried to the guard, as he lifted me inside.

The door was closed. Thus was I separated from Bessie and Gateshead, thus carried away to unknown and, as it then seemed to me, far-off and mysterious places.

I remember but little of the journey. I only know that the day seemed endless, and that we appeared to travel over hundreds of miles of road. We passed through several towns, and in one large one the coach stopped, the horses were taken out, and the passengers descended to dine. I was carried into an inn, where the guard wanted me to have some food, but I had no appetite. He left me in an immense room, where I walked up and down, greatly afraid of someone coming and taking me away, for I had heard about children being stolen in many of Bessie's stories.

We continued on our way. The wet, misty afternoon changed to twilight. We ceased to pass through towns, the scenery altered, and great grey hills appeared on the horizon. We descended a valley, dark with woods.

At last I fell asleep, but soon the stopping of the coach awoke me. The door was open, and a person was standing by it. I saw her face and dress by the light of the lamps.

"Is there a little girl called Jane Eyre here?" she asked. I answered "Yes," and was lifted out. My trunk was handed down, and the coach instantly drove away.

I was stiff with long sitting, and confused with the noise and movement of the coach. Gathering up my senses, I looked about me. Rain, wind and darkness filled the air. However, I dimly observed a wall before me, and a door open in it. Through this door I passed with my new guide. A house with many windows, in some of which lights were burning, was now visible. We went up a broad path and were admitted at a door, then I was led through a passage into a room with a fire, and left alone.

CHAPTER 6

LOWOOD INSTITUTION

AFTER warming my frozen fingers over the blaze, I looked round. It was a sitting-room, not so splendid as the drawing-room at Gateshead, but comfortable enough.

A tall lady entered, followed by another.

" The child is very young to be sent alone," said the first. She looked at me for a minute, and then added: " She had better be put to bed soon; she looks tired. Are you tired? " She placed her hand on my shoulder as she spoke.

" A little, ma'am."

" And hungry too, no doubt. Let her have some supper before she goes to bed, Miss Miller. Is this the first time you have left your parents to come to school, my little girl? "

I explained that I had no parents. She asked how long they had been dead, then my age, my name, and whether I could read, write and sew a little. Then she touched my cheek gently with her finger, and saying that she hoped I should be a good child, dismissed me with Miss Miller.

The lady whom we now left was (as I afterwards learnt) Miss Temple, the head mistress. Miss Miller looked younger, but more ordinary. She seemed tired. Led by her, I passed through rooms and passages till I heard the hum of many voices and shortly after entered a wide, long room with great tables, two at each end, on each of which burnt a pair of candles. Seated all round was a collection of girls of every age, from nine or ten to twenty. They were all dressed in brown. It was the hour of study, and they were preparing their work for the next day.

Miss Miller made a sign to me to sit down, then walking to the top of the long room, she cried out:

" Monitors,[1] collect the lesson-books and put them away."

[1] monitor = a pupil chosen to do some special duty, e.g., collect exercise books.

Four tall girls arose from different tables, and going round, gathered the books and removed them. Miss Miller again gave the word of command:

"Monitors, fetch the supper-trays."[1]

The tall girls went out and returned presently, each bearing a tray, with pieces of bread arranged on it, and a jug[2] of water and a cup in the middle. The bread was handed round, and those who wanted took a drink of water. When it came to my turn I drank, for I was thirsty, but I was too tired to eat.

The meal being over, prayers were said, and the classes moved off in order, two by two, upstairs. Overcome with weariness, I scarcely noticed what sort of a place the bedroom was, except that like the schoolroom it was very long. Miss Miller helped me to undress. Each of the long rows of beds was quickly filled, and in ten minutes the single light was put out.

The night passed rapidly. I was too tired even to dream. When I opened my eyes a loud bell was ringing. The girls were up and dressing. Day had not yet begun to dawn, and a light burned in the room. I, too, rose and dressed unwillingly. It was bitterly cold, I washed when there was a basin at liberty, which did not occur soon, for there was only one basin to every six girls. Again the bell rang. All formed in line, two by two, and in that order descended the stairs, and entered the cold and dimly lit schoolroom. Here prayers were said, and Miss Miller afterwards called out:

"Form classes."

A great amount of noise and movement followed for some minutes, during which Miss Miller repeatedly exclaimed: "Silence!" and "Order!" When it had ceased, I saw that the girls were arranged in four half-circles, each before a table and chair. All held books in their hands, and a great book lay on each table. A pause of some moments followed. Miss Miller walked from class to class, silencing the whisperers.

---

[1] tray = a flat piece of wood or metal, on which cups, glasses, etc., are carried.
[2] jug = a container for water.

A distant bell sounded. Immediately three ladies entered the room; each walked to a table, and Miss Miller took the fourth one, round which the smallest children were assembled. To this inferior class I was now called, and placed at the bottom of it.

Work now began with a lengthy reading of the Bible. By the time that was over, day had fully dawned. The bell sounded once more; the classes were marched into another room for breakfast. How glad I was at the thought of getting something to eat! I was now nearly sick from emptiness, having taken so little the day before.

The dining-room tables were set with steaming basins of something hot, but to my disappointment the smell was not inviting. I saw universal signs of discontent, and from the front of the procession the tall girls in the first class began to murmur:

" Disgusting! The porridge[1] is burnt again! "

A prayer was said, then a servant brought in some tea for the teachers, and the meal began.

Violently hungry, and now very faint, I eagerly ate a spoonful of my helping without thinking of the taste, but when I had satisfied the first sharpness of hunger I could eat no more. All around me the spoons moved slowly: I saw each girl taste her food and try to swallow it, but in most cases the attempt was soon given up.

Another prayer having been said, we returned to the schoolroom. I was one of the last to go out, and in passing the tables, I saw one of the teachers take a basin of porridge and taste it. She looked at the others. All their faces expressed displeasure.

A quarter of an hour passed before lessons began again, during which everyone talked loudly and freely. Every conversation was about the breakfast. I heard the name of Mr. Brocklehurst pronounced by some, at which Miss Miller shook her head disapprovingly, but she made no attempt to check the general complaints. No doubt she sympathized with us.

[1] porridge = a breakfast food made from a kind of grain.

At nine o'clock there was a sudden silence. The head mistress had entered. She summoned the first class around her and gave a geography lesson. The lower classes worked with the other teachers at history and grammar, then writing and arithmetic followed, and music lessons were given to some of the elder girls by Miss Temple.

At last the clock struck twelve. The head mistress rose.

"I have a word to address to the pupils," she said. "You had this morning a breakfast which you could not eat. You must be hungry. I have ordered that a meal of bread and cheese shall be served to all."

The teachers looked at her with surprise.

"It is to be done on my responsibility," she added, and immediately afterwards left the room.

The bread and cheese was soon brought in and handed round, to the delight of the whole school. The order was then given: "To the garden!" Following the crowd, I found my way into the open air.

The garden was a wide enclosure within high walls. A middle space was divided into numerous little squares, which were given to each pupil as gardens to cultivate. When full of flowers they would doubtless look pretty, but now all was wintry. The stronger of the girls ran about and played games, but many pale and thin ones herded together for shelter and warmth in a covered space at the end, and these I often heard coughing in the damp and misty air.

I had not yet spoken to anyone, nor did anybody take any notice of me. I stood lonely enough, but I was used to being apart from others. I leaned against a pillar of the shelter and watched, trying to forget the cold. I looked up at the house. Over the door the following words were cut in stone:

LOWOOD INSTITUTION. THIS BUILDING WAS ESTABLISHED BY
NAOMI BROCKLEHURST, OF BROCKLEHURST HALL.

I read these words over, and as I did so a cough sounded behind me. I turned my head and saw a girl sitting on a seat reading. In turning over a page she happened to look up, and I said to her directly:

" Is your book interesting? "

" I like it," she answered after a pause of a second or two in which she examined me.

" What is it about? "

" You may look at it," replied the girl, offering me the book.

I too liked reading, but I soon saw that this was too difficult for me. I returned it to her, and she received it quietly. She was about to go on with her story, but again I ventured to disturb her.

" Can you tell me what the writing on that stone over the door means? What is Lowood Institution? "

" This house that you have come to live in. I suppose you are an orphan, are you not? "

" Both my parents died before I can remember."

" Well, all the girls in this school have lost their parents. This is an institution for educating orphans."

" Do we pay no money? Do they keep us for nothing? "

" We pay, or our friends pay, fifteen pounds a year for each. It is not enough, and the rest is supplied by generous ladies and gentlemen in this neighbourhood and in London."

" Who is Naomi Brocklehurst? "

" The lady who built most of this house, and whose son controls and directs everything here."

" Then this house does not belong to the tall lady who said we were to have some bread and cheese? "

" To Miss Temple? Oh, no! I wish it did. She is responsible to Mr. Brocklehurst for all she does. He buys all our food and clothes."

" Is he a good man? "

" He is a clergyman."

" Do you like the teachers? "

" Well enough."

I asked for their names and characters, how long she had been at the school, and finally, whether she was happy there

"You ask rather too many questions. Now I want to read."

But at that moment the bell rang, and all re-entered the house. Dinner was served in two huge tin dishes, from which rose a strong smell of bad fat, not much better than that at breakfast-time. The mixture consisted of not very good potatoes and strange bits of greasy brown meat cooked together. I ate what I could, and wondered whether the meals would be like this every day.

After dinner, there were more lessons till five o'clock.

The only event of the afternoon was that I saw the girl with whom I had conversed dismissed in disgrace from a history class, and sent to stand in the middle of the large classroom. The punishment seemed to me deeply humiliating, especially for so big a girl—she looked thirteen years or more. To my surprise she neither wept nor blushed.

"How can she bear it so quietly?" I asked myself. "She looks as if she were thinking of something beyond her punishment. She is looking at what she can remember, not what is really present. I wonder what sort of a girl she is—whether good or naughty."

Soon after five, we had another meal, consisting of a small cup of coffee, and half a piece of brown bread. I ate eagerly, but I remained hungry. Half an hour's play followed, then study, then the cup of water and bread, prayers, and bed. Such was my first day at Lowood.

CHAPTER 7

HELEN BURNS

THE next day began as before, with getting up and dressing before sunrise, but this morning we were obliged to do without washing, the water in the jugs was frozen.

Before the long hour of Bible-reading was over, I felt ready to perish with cold. Breakfast-time came at last, and this morning the porridge was not burnt. The quality was eatable, but the quantity small. How tiny my helping seemed! I wished it were doubled!

In the course of the day I began work as a member of the fourth class. At first, being little accustomed to learn by heart, the lessons appeared to me both long and difficult. The frequent change from one subject to another, too, confused me, and I was glad when at about three o'clock in the afternoon Miss Smith put some sewing into my hands and sent me to sit in a quiet corner of the schoolroom. At that hour most of the others were also sewing, but one class still stood round a teacher reading, and as all was quiet, the subject of their lesson could be heard, together with the answers of the pupils and the criticisms of the teacher. It was history, and I observed my acquaintance of the day before at the top of the class, until for some error she was sent to the very bottom. Even then she was constantly scolded in such words as these:

" Burns (such was her name: the girls here were all called by their surnames[1])—you are standing on the side of your shoe; turn your toes out immediately." " Burns, hold your head up."

A chapter having been read through twice, the books were closed and the girls examined. Most of them seemed to find it difficult, but Burns was ready with answers at every point. I kept expecting Miss Scatcherd, the teacher, to praise her, but instead she suddenly cried out:

" You dirty, disagreeable girl! You have not cleaned your nails this morning! "

Burns made no answer: I was surprised at her silence.

" Why," I thought, " does she not explain that the water was frozen this morning? "

My attention was now called for by Miss Smith, who wanted to look at my work. When I returned to my seat, Burns was just leaving the room in obedience to some order from Miss Scatcherd. She returned in half a minute carrying in her hand a bundle of sticks tied together at one end. This she presented to the teacher respectfully. Miss Scatcherd in-

---

[1] surname = family name.

stantly and sharply struck a dozen blows on her neck. Not a tear rose to Burns' eye, and while I paused from my sewing, because my fingers trembled with anger at this scene, not a feature of her thoughtful face altered its expression.

During the play-hour that evening, I made my way to the fireplace. There, kneeling by it, I found Burns, her attention fixed on a book.

"Is that the same one as yesterday?" I asked.

"Yes, I have just finished it." She shut it up.

"What is your name besides Burns?"

"Helen."

"Do you come from far away?"

"I come from a place farther north, on the borders of Scotland."

"You must wish to leave Lowood."

"No, why should I? I was sent here to get an education, and it would be of no use going away before I had done so."

"But that teacher, Miss Scatcherd, is so cruel to you."

"Cruel? Not at all! She is severe; she dislikes my faults."

"If I were in your place, and she struck me, I should get the rod from her hand and break it under her nose."

"If you did, Mr. Brocklehurst would expel you from the school, and that would be a great grief to your relations."

"But it seems to me disgraceful to be beaten in front of everyone. I could not bear it."

"It is weak and silly to say that you cannot bear what it is necessary for you to bear."

I heard her with wonder: I could not understand her point of view.

"You say you have faults, Helen: what are they? To me you seem very good."

"I am, as Miss Scatcherd says, careless and untidy. I seldom keep things in order. I forget rules. I read when I should be learning my lessons."

"Is Miss Temple as severe to you as Miss Scatcherd?"

A soft smile came over her face.

"Miss Temple is full of goodness. She sees my faults, and tells me them gently. When I do anything, she praises me generously."

"And when Miss Temple teaches you, do your thoughts wander?"

"No, not often, because what she says is generally so interesting to me."

"You are good to those who are good to you. That is all I ever desire to be. But when we are struck without a reason, we should strike back very hard."

"It is not violence that best overcomes hate. The good try to love their enemies, and bless those that curse them."

"Then I should love Mrs. Reed, and bless her son John, which is impossible."

In her turn Helen asked me to explain, and I poured out the story of my past sufferings. She heard me patiently to the end, but said nothing.

"Well," I asked, "is not Mrs. Reed a bad, hard-hearted woman?"

"She has been unkind to you, no doubt, but would you not be happier if you tried to forget her severity? Life appears to me to be too short to be spent in remembering past injustices."

I saw by Helen's look that she no longer wished to talk, but rather to be left with her thoughts. This, however, was not permitted for long. A monitor came up, a great rough girl, exclaiming:

"Helen Burns, if you don't go and put your drawer tidy this minute, I'll tell Miss Scatcherd to come and look at it!"

Helen got up and obeyed without delay.

CHAPTER 8

A VISIT FROM MR. BROCKLEHURST

ONE afternoon when I had been about three weeks at Lowood, I was sitting puzzling over some arithmetic. Suddenly the whole school, including the teachers, rose, and I saw standing beside Miss Temple the same black pillar that had looked at me so severely in the breakfast-room at Gateshead.

All the time I had been dreading the fulfilment of Mr. Brocklehurst's promise to Mrs. Reed. Now he was speaking in a low voice to the head mistress. Was it about me? I was near enough to hear some of his words, and for the moment I felt relieved.

" I wish the woollen stockings to be looked after better. When I was here last I examined the clothes hanging out to dry. There were many holes in the stockings."

" Your instructions shall be attended to, sir," said Miss Temple.

" And, ma'am," he continued, " I find that some of the girls have two clean collars in the week. It is too much : the rule limits them to one."

" I think I can explain that circumstance, sir. Two of the pupils were invited to take tea with some friends last Thursday, and I gave them permission to put on clean collars for the occasion."

Mr. Brocklehurst nodded.

" Well, for once it may be allowed, but please do not let it occur too often. And there is another thing which surprised me. I find, in looking at the accounts with the housekeeper that a meal, consisting of bread and cheese, has been served out to the girls during the last month. How is this? No such meal is mentioned in the school rules. Who introduced this change? And by what authority? "

" I must be responsible for the circumstance, sir," replied Miss Temple. " The breakfast was so badly cooked that the pupils could not possibly eat it; and I dared not allow them to remain without food till dinner-time."

" Madam, you are aware that my plan in bringing up these girls is not to accustom them to habits of rich living. Should any little accidental disappointment of the appetite occur, they should be encouraged to suffer the hardship without complaint."

Miss Temple. gazed straight before her, her face showing nothing of her feelings. Meanwhile Mr. Brocklehurst, with his hands behind his back, let his eyes travel over the whole school. Suddenly he closed them for a moment, as if they had met something that shocked them. Turning, he spoke more rapidly than before:

"Miss Temple, Miss Temple, has that girl got curled hair? Red hair, ma'am, curled all over!" And he pointed at it with his stick, his hand shaking.

"Julia's hair curls naturally," returned Miss Temple quietly.

"I have again and again stated that I desire the girls' hair to be arranged closely, modestly, plainly. Miss Temple, that girl's hair must be cut off; I will send a barber to-morrow. And I see others who have far too much. Tell all the first class to turn their faces to the wall."

Miss Temple pressed her handkerchief to her lips, as if to hide the smile that formed there. She gave the order, how-ever. Leaning back a little on my seat, I could see the dis-satisfied looks on the girls' faces. Mr. Brocklehurst examined the backs of their heads for five minutes, and then gave the order:

"All that hair must come off."

Miss Temple seemed about to object, but she was interrupted by the arrival of three other visitors, ladies clothed in silk and furs. They ought to have come a little sooner to have heard the gentleman's remarks, for their hair was arranged in masses of curls. These ladies were the wife and daughters of Mr. Brocklehurst, and they had been examining the bedrooms, and had many complaints to make.

Till now, while watching with the greatest interest the scene before me, I had not neglected to think of my personal safety. I had sat well back on my seat, and had held my book in such a manner as to hide my face. I might have escaped notice, had not my book happened to slip from my hand, and falling with a loud crash, instantly drawn every eye upon me.

"A careless girl!" said Mr. Brocklehurst. "It is the new

pupil, I observe. I must not forget that I have a word to say about her. Let the child come forward."

I could not have moved by myself, but two elder girls set me on my legs and pushed me towards the dreadful judge.

" Fetch that chair, and place the child upon it."

It was a very high one, and I was now on a level with Mr. Brocklehurst's face.

" Ladies," he said, " Miss Temple, teachers and children, you all see this girl? She is very young. Who would think that she was already a servant of the Devil? You must keep away from her. Avoid her company, do not play with her or speak to her. Teachers, you must watch her, examine well her words and actions. For this girl, this child, is a liar! "

Now came a pause, during which all the female Brocklehursts shook their heads and said: " How shocking! "

Mr. Brocklehurst continued.

" This I learnt from her guardian, the generous lady who adopted her and brought her up as her own daughter, until she became so ungrateful that the excellent lady was obliged to separate her from her own children, for fear that her bad behaviour might affect them."

He moved towards the door with his family. Turning at the last moment he said:

" Let her stand half an hour longer on that chair, and let no one speak to her for the rest of the day."

There was I, who had said that I could not bear the shame of standing in the middle of the room, now publicly disgraced. No words can describe my feelings. But just as they began to get beyond my control, Helen passed by me, and in passing, lifted her eyes and smiled. In some strange way she filled me with her own courage. I mastered my emotion, lifted my head, and took a firm stand on the chair.

CHAPTER 9

MISS TEMPLE

BEFORE the half-hour ended, the bell rang. School was over, and all went into the dining-room for tea. I now ventured to descend and creep into a corner. The courage that had supported me was beginning to fade, and I was so overcome with grief that I sank down with my face on the ground. I wept. I had meant to be so good, to do so much at Lowood, to make so many friends, to deserve respect and affection. Already I had made progress in class and received praise from my teacher, and I was well liked by my fellow-pupils and treated as an equal by those of my own age. But now all hope was over, and I could only wish to die.

Someone approached: it was Helen Burns. She brought me my coffee and bread.

" Come, eat something," she said, but I put both away from me, and continued to weep aloud.

" Helen, why do you stay with a girl whom everybody believes to be a liar, and whom everybody despises? "

" Jane, you are mistaken: probably not one in the school either dislikes or despises you. Many, I am sure, pity you."

" How can they pity me after what Mr. Brocklehurst has said? "

" Mr. Brocklehurst is not a god, nor is he even a great and admired man. He is little liked here. Had he treated you with special favour you would have found enemies; as it is, most of the girls would offer you sympathy if they dared. Teachers and pupils may look coldly on you for a day or two, but there are friendly feelings in their hearts. Besides, Jane . . ." She paused.

" Well, Helen? "

" If all the world hated you, and believed you wicked, while your own conscience approved of you, you could still hold up your head."

39

I was silent. Helen had calmed me. Resting my head on her shoulder, I put my arm round her waist. We had not sat long thus when Miss Temple came in.

" I came on purpose to find you, Jane Eyre," she said. " I want you in my room, and as Helen Burns is with you she may come too."

We followed her to her sitting-room, where she called me to her side.

" Is it all over? " she asked, looking down at my face. " Have you cried your sorrow away? "

" I shall never do that."

" Why? "

" Because I have been wrongly accused, and you, ma'am, and everybody else, will think me to be wicked."

" We shall think you what you prove yourself to be, my child. Continue to act as a good girl, and you will satisfy us."

" Shall I, Miss Temple? "

" You will. Now, Jane, you know that when a criminal is accused, he is always allowed to speak in his own defence You have been charged with telling lies; defend yourself to me as well as you can. Say whatever your memory suggests to be true, but add nothing."

Thus encouraged, I reflected for a few minutes and having arranged my story in order, I told her the history of my childhood. As I went on I felt that she fully believed me.

In the course of the tale I had mentioned Mr. Lloyd as having come to see me during my illness. When I had finished, Miss Temple looked at me for a few minutes in silence. She then said :

" I know Mr. Lloyd. I shall write to him. If his reply is satisfactory, you shall be publicly cleared. To me, you are cleared now."

She kissed me, and still keeping me by her side, where I was well content to stand, went on to address Helen Burns.

" How are you to-night, Helen? Have you coughed much to-day? "

" Not quite so much, ma'am, I think."

" And the pain in your chest? "

" It is a little better."

Miss Temple looked thoughtful for a few minutes, then she rang the bell and ordered tea. Having invited Helen and me to approach the table and drink, she unlocked a cupboard and brought out a good-sized cake. She looked on with a satisfied smile as we enjoyed the food, so rare and delicious to us.

After tea, she again summoned us to the fire. We sat on either side of her, and I listened with respect and admiration to the conversation between her and Helen. The meal, the bright fire, the presence of her dearly loved teacher, seemed to have roused Helen and broken down her silence. Her fine features looked full of life, and her intelligent eyes flashed as she and Miss Temple conversed of things I had never heard of, of nations and times past, of countries far away, of books and authors. What stores of knowledge they possessed! How many books they had read!

All too soon the bell rang for bedtime. No delay could be admitted. Miss Temple kissed us both, saying as she did so:

" God bless you, my children! "

About a week after these events, Miss Temple, having assembled the whole school, announced that an inquiry had been made into the charges against Jane Eyre, and that she was most happy to be able to declare her completely cleared. The teachers then shook hands with me, and a murmur of pleasure ran through the rows of my companions.

I was thus relieved of a heavy load; from that hour I set to work once more. I studied hard, and was rewarded with success. My memory improved, and in a few weeks I was moved to a higher class. In less than two months I was allowed to begin French and drawing. My ambition was now roused, and in spite of the daily hardships, I would not have exchanged Lowood for all the comforts of Gateshead.

CHAPTER 10

THE DEATH OF HELEN

As spring advanced, the hardships of Lowood lessened. The frosts of winter ceased, the snows melted, the sharp winds grew milder. We could now enjoy the play-hour passed in the garden. On Thursday afternoons (half-holidays) we now went for walks, and I learnt for the first time to take pleasure in fine scenery, in the hills that enclosed our wooded valley. Trees, flowers, and the rushing streams all delighted me.

But although the neighbourhood was pleasant, it was unhealthy. Before May arrived, a fever had attacked the crowded schoolroom and turned the orphanage into a hospital. Insufficient food and neglected colds made most of the pupils liable to catch the disease easily: forty-five out of the eighty girls lay ill at one time. Classes were broken up, rules were forgotten. The few who continued well were allowed almost unlimited freedom, because the doctor insisted on the necessity for frequent exercise to keep them in health. Miss Temple's whole attention was taken up by the patients. The teachers were fully occupied in helping those girls who were fortunate enough to have friends and relations willing to remove them from danger, to pack and leave. Many departed only to die.

But I, and the rest who continued well, did what we liked and went where we liked. Mr. Brocklehurst and his family never came near Lowood now. We lived for whole days out-of-doors.

And where, meanwhile, was Helen Burns?. She was ill. For some weeks she had been removed from my sight to some room upstairs. She was not, I was told, in the same part of the house as the fever patients, for her illness was a disease of the lungs. I, in my ignorance, understood this to be something mild, which time and care would be sure to cure. The idea was strengthened in my mind by the fact that she once or twice came downstairs on very warm sunny afternoons, and was taken by Miss Temple into the garden; but I was not allowed to go and speak to her.

One evening the doctor appeared at an unusual hour, a sign that someone was very ill. I was near the front door when he left, and I ran up to the nurse who had been speaking to him.

"How is Helen Burns?"

"Very weak," was the answer.

"What does the doctor say about her?"

"He says she'll not be here long"

At ordinary times I should have taken this sentence to mean merely that Helen was going to her own home. I should not have suspected that it meant that she was dying, but I knew instantly now. I felt a shock of horror, then a strong grief, then a desire, a need to see her. I asked in which room she lay.

"She is in Miss Temple's room," said the nurse.

"May I go up and speak to her?"

"No, child."

It was just nine o'clock, and Miss Miller was calling the pupils to go to bed. I went with the rest.

Two hours later, I rose softly and crept without shoes in search of Miss Temple's room. It was at the other end of the house, but I knew my way. I passed quickly by the fever room, fearful lest the nurse who sat up all night should hear me.

Close by Miss Temple's bed, stood a smaller one. I saw the outline of a form under the clothes. The nurse to whom I had spoken in the garden was sitting in a chair asleep. Miss Temple was not to be seen: I learnt afterwards that she had been called to the bedside of another patient. I advanced.

"Helen!" I whispered softly, "are you awake?"

She stirred, and I saw her pale, calm face.

"Is it you, Jane?" she asked, in her own gentle voice.

"Oh!" I thought, "she is not going to die. They are mistaken: she could not speak and look so calmly if she were."

" Why have you come here, Jane? It is past eleven o'clock: I heard the clock strike some minutes ago."

" I came to see you, Helen. I heard you were very ill, and I could not sleep until I had spoken to you."

" You came to say good-bye to me, then. You are just in time, probably."

" Are you going somewhere, Helen? "

" Yes, to my last home."

" No, no, Helen! " I stopped, overcome by my feelings. While I tried to keep back my tears, Helen began to cough. After a long silence, she whispered:

" I am very happy, Jane, and when you hear that I am dead, you must not be sad. We must all die one day, and the illness which is removing me is gentle and gradual. My mind is at rest. I leave no one to regret me much. I have only a father, and he has lately re-married, and will not miss me. I am going to God."

Presently she added:

" How comfortable I am! That last attack of coughing has tired me a little: I feel as if I could sleep. Don't leave me, Jane, I like to have you near me."

" I'll stay with you, dear Helen; no one shall take me away."

I lay down beside her. She kissed me, and we both soon slept.

When I awoke it was day, and Helen was . . . dead.

CHAPTER 11

ADVERTISEMENT FOR A POST

THE fever gradually disappeared from Lowood, but not before its violence and the number of sufferers had drawn public attention to the school. Inquiry was made into the cause of the outbreak, and various facts came to light which roused public anger to the highest degree. The unhealthy position of the building, the quantity and quality of the children's food, the impure water supply, the pupils' miserable clothing and crowded living space—all these things were discovered, and the discovery brought disgrace to Mr. Brocklehurst, but benefits to the school.

Several wealthy individuals in the district combined to pay for the building of a better establishment in a healthier situation. New rules were made, improvements in food and clothing were introduced, and the control of the school was put into the hands of a committee. Mr. Brocklehurst still kept his post of treasurer, but his activities were watched by more generous-minded gentlemen. The school, thus improved, became in time a truly useful place.

I remained in it for eight years. During this time my life was without change, but I was not unhappy, because I was not inactive. I had the chance of an excellent education. A fondness for some of my studies, and a desire to do my best in all, together with a great delight in pleasing my teachers, urged me on. In time I rose to be the first girl in the first class; then for two years I became a teacher.

Miss Temple had till now continued as head mistress of Lowood. To her instruction I owed the better part of my education, while her friendship and company had been my continual source of contentment. She had stood for me in the place of mother, teacher and friend. But at this period she married; she left with her husband for a distant part of the country, and was lost to me.

From that day, I was no longer the same. My world had been for some years the narrow one of Lowood, and now that it seemed empty, I remembered that the real world was wide, and offered a varied life to those who had the courage to go out into it. My holidays had all been spent at Lowood, and neither Mrs. Reed nor her family had ever written to me or come to see me. School rules, school duties, school habits—such was all I knew. A sudden wild longing for liberty came over me.

"What do I want?" I asked myself. "A new place, in a new house, among new faces, in new circumstances is the best

I can hope for. How do people get a new place? They apply to friends, I suppose. I have no friends. What do people do in such a case? "

I could not tell: nothing answered me. But after a night's sleep an idea came quietly and naturally to my mind. I must advertise.

I was up very early. I had my advertisement written before the bell rang to rouse the school. It was as follows:

A young lady accustomed to teaching desires to find a post in a private family where the children are under fourteen. She is qualified to teach the usual subjects of a good English education, together with French, drawing and music. Address, J.E., Post Office, Lowton.

After tea, I asked permission of the new head mistress to go to the neighbouring town of Lowton. It was readily granted. I went, visited a shop or two, slipped my letter to the newspaper into the post-office box, and returned home with a relieved heart.

The next week seemed long, but at last it ended, and I went once more into the town. The post office was kept by an old lady, who wore spectacles on her nose.

" Are there any letters for J.E.? " I asked.

She gazed at me over her glasses, then opened a drawer, and turned over its contents so long that I began to despair. At last, having held a letter for nearly five minutes in front of her spectacles, she passed it over, accompanying the act by a curious and distrustful look.

" Is there only one? " I demanded.

" There are no more," she answered.

I put it in my pocket and hurried back. Duties awaited me at school: I had to sit with the girls during their study hour, then it was my turn to say prayers, and to see the school to bed. It was night before I was free to open my letter. The contents were brief.

If J.E., who advertised last Thursday, possesses the qualifications mentioned, and if she is able to give satisfactory evidence as to character, a situation can be offered her where there is only one pupil, a little girl, under ten years of age. The salary is thirty pounds a year. J.E. is requested to reply to Mrs. Fairfax, Thornfield, near Millcote.

I examined the letter for a long time. The writing was old-fashioned and rather hesitating, like that of an elderly[1] lady. This circumstance was satisfactory: it sounded respectable.[2] The salary mentioned was twice what I was earning.

Next day I made known my intention to the head mistress, and asked her to mention the matter to the committee, or to Mr. Brocklehurst, and find out whether they would support my application. Mr. Brocklehurst declared that Mrs. Reed must be written to, as my natural guardian. A letter was accordingly sent to that lady, who returned for answer that I might do as I pleased, as she had long given up any interest in my affairs. This reply went to the committee, and at last formal permission was given to me to better my condition, and a letter of recommendation, signed by the inspectors, was presented.

I sent a copy of this letter to Mrs. Fairfax, and got that lady's reply, stating that she was satisfied, and fixing the date when I should take up my duties as governess[3] in her house.

CHAPTER 12

AT THORNFIELD

I WAS quite alone in the world—a strange feeling for an inexperienced girl.

I had left Lowton at four o'clock in the morning, and now, at eight o'clock in the same evening, I was at the George Inn at Millcote, waiting to be met and taken to Thornfield. The

---

[1] elderly = rather old.
[2] respectable = of good reputation, worthy of respect.
[3] governess = a lady who looks after and teaches children in a private family.

first feeling of adventure had given place to one of fear, and all sorts of doubts were troubling me.

After half an hour, I rang the bell.

" Is there a place in this neighbourhood called Thornfield? " I asked the waiter who answered my call.

" Thornfield? I don't know, ma'am: I'll inquire." He went away, but reappeared almost immediately.

" Is your name Eyre, miss? "

" Yes."

" There is a person waiting for you."

A man was standing at the entrance to the inn, and in the lamp-lit street I dimly saw a one-horse carriage.

" I suppose," I thought, " judging from the plainness of the servant and the carriage, Mrs. Fairfax is not a very fashionable person. All the better for me. I have only once lived amongst fine people, and I was very miserable with them. I wonder if she lives alone except for this little girl. I pray God she may not be like Mrs. Reed, but if she is, I am not compelled to stay with her. If I am not satisfied, I can advertise again."

The roads were heavy, the night misty. My driver let his horse walk all the way. It was two hours before he got down and opened a pair of gates. We passed through, slowly ascended an avenue, and came to the long front of a house. The door was opened by a maid-servant.

" Will you walk this way, ma'am? " said the girl. I followed her across a square hall, and she showed me into a room which offered an agreeable picture to my view.

It was a comfortable, small room. There was a round table by a cheerful fire, and a high-backed, old-fashioned armchair, in which sat the neatest little elderly lady, in widow's cap, black silk dress, and snowy white apron. She was occupied in sewing, and a large cat sat at her feet. A more encouraging introduction for a new governess could scarcely be imagined. As I entered, the old lady got up and came forward to meet me.

" How do you do, my dear? I am afraid you have had a long drive. John drives so slowly. You must be cold: come to the fire."

" Mrs. Fairfax, I suppose? "

" Yes, you are right: do sit down."

She led me to her own chair, and then began to remove my coat. I begged she would not give herself so much trouble. She then ordered me a hot drink, and went off to see that my luggage was carried to my room.

" She treats me like a visitor," I thought. " This is not like what I have heard of the treatment of governesses."

I felt rather confused at being the object of more attention than I had ever before received, and that, too, shown by my employer and superior.

" Shall I have the pleasure of seeing Miss Fairfax to-night? " I asked.

" Miss Fairfax? Oh, you mean Miss Adele Varens! Varens is the name of your future pupil."

" Indeed! Then she is not your daughter? "

" No—I have no family. I am so glad you have come," she continued. " It will be quite pleasant living here now with a companion. In the winter one feels so gloomy alone with only the servants. But I'll not keep you sitting up late to-night: it is nearly twelve now, and you have been travelling all day."

She took her candle, and after seeing that the front door was fastened, led the way upstairs. A very cold air filled the dark staircase and the long passage, and I was glad to find that my own room was small, and furnished in ordinary modern style.

CHAPTER 13

STRANGE LAUGHTER

My room the next morning looked bright and gay in the sunlight, with papered walls and a carpeted floor, so unlike the bare wood and stained plaster of Lowood that I grew cheerful at the sight. Perhaps a happier time of life was beginning for me.

I rose and dressed myself with care. Both my clothes and looks were plain, but I was neat by nature, and my black dress fitted me well.

Going downstairs, I found the hall door open, and stepped outside. It was a fine autumn morning, and advancing on to the lawn, I looked up and examined the front of the house. It was three storeys[1] high, and of great size.

I was enjoying the pleasant fresh air when Mrs. Fairfax appeared at the door.

"What! Out already?" she said. "I feel you are an early riser. How do you like Thornfield?"

I told her that I liked it very much.

"Yes," she said, "it is a pretty place, but I fear it will be getting out of order, unless Mr. Rochester should decide to come and live here permanently."

"Mr. Rochester!" I exclaimed. "Who is he?"

"The owner of Thornfield," she replied quietly.

"But I thought that Thornfield belonged to you."

"To me? Bless you, child; what an idea! I am only the housekeeper."

"And the little girl—my pupil?"

"Mr. Rochester is her guardian. He asked me to find her a governess. Here she comes, with her nurse."

The mystery, then, was explained. This kind little widow was no great lady, and the equality between her and me was real. I felt better pleased than ever.

As I was thinking over this discovery, a little girl came running up. She was perhaps seven or eight years old, with a pale, small-featured face, and hair falling in curls to her waist.

"Good morning, Miss Adele," said Mrs. Fairfax. "Come and speak to the lady who is to teach you."

She approached. "Is that my governess?" she said in French, pointing to me, and addressing her nurse, who answered in the same language:

"Yes, certainly."

[1] storey = a set of rooms in a house all on the same level. The first storey is on the ground, the second above the first, and so on.

" Are they foreigners? " I inquired.

" The nurse is a foreigner, and Adele was born in Paris, and, I believe, never left it till six months ago. When she first came here she could speak no English, but now she can talk it a little."

Fortunately I had had the advantage of being taught French by a French lady, and had practised conversation with her as often as I could. I immediately addressed my pupil in her own language, and she was soon talking happily to me at the breakfast-table.

After the meal, Adele and I went to the library, which Mr. Rochester had ordered to be used as the schoolroom. I found my pupil obedient, but not used to regular occupation of any kind. I felt it would be unwise to be too strict with her at first, so when I had got her to learn a little, and it was near midday, I allowed her to return to her nurse.

As I was going upstairs, Mrs. Fairfax addressed me from across the hall:

" Your morning school hours are over now, I suppose."

I went into the room she was tidying.

" What a beautiful room! " I exclaimed, as I looked round.

" Yes, this is the dining-room. I have just opened the windows to admit a little air and sunshine. Everything gets so damp in rooms that are seldom inhabited."

" In what good order you keep these rooms, Mrs. Fairfax! "

" Why, Miss Eyre, though Mr. Rochester's visits here are rare, they are always sudden and unexpected, and he dislikes not finding everything ready to receive him."

" Is Mr. Rochester hard to please? "

" Not particularly, but he has a gentleman's tastes and habits."

" But has he no peculiarities? "

" He is rather peculiar, perhaps. He has travelled a great deal, and seen a great deal of the world. I suppose he is clever, but I have never had much conversation with him. It is not easy to describe, but you cannot be sure, when he speaks to you, whether he is joking or in earnest."

This was all the account I got from the simple old lady of her employer and mine.

When we left the dining-room, she proposed to show me over the rest of the house, and I followed her upstairs and downstairs, admiring as I went. The large front rooms I thought especially grand and some of the third storey rooms, though dark and low, contained interesting old furniture.

" Do the servants sleep in these rooms? " I asked.

" No, they occupy a set of smaller rooms at the back."

" You have no ghost here, I suppose? "

" None that I ever heard of," returned Mrs. Fairfax, smiling. " Will you come and see the view from the roof? "

I followed up a narrow staircase and a ladder. As I looked down, the neighbourhood lay beneath me like a map: lawn, fields, woods, the church at the gates, the road, the village, the quiet hills.

While I descended, Mrs. Fairfax stayed behind for a moment to fasten the door on to the roof. I reached the third storey, and waited in the long passage separating the front and back rooms. It was narrow, low and dim, with only one window at the far end.

As I walked on softly, I heard a most unexpected sound in so still a place—a laugh. It was a curious laugh; distinct, un-natural, not at all merry. I stopped. The sound ceased, but only for an instant. Then it began again, louder. It passed off in a noisy burst that seemed to echo in every lonely room.

" Mrs. Fairfax! " I called out, for I now heard her descend-ing the stairs. " Did you hear that loud laugh? Who is it? "

" Some of the servants, very likely," she answered. " Per-haps Grace Poole. She sews in one of these rooms. Some-times another maid is with her: they are frequently noisy together."

The laugh was repeated in its low tone, and ended in an odd murmur.

" Grace! " exclaimed Mrs. Fairfax.

I really did not expect anyone to answer, for the laugh was both despairing and ghostly. However, the door nearest to me opened, and a servant came out—a woman between thirty and forty, with a square figure, and a hard, plain face. Nothing more ordinary could be imagined.

"Too much noise, Grace," said Mrs. Fairfax. "Remember instructions!" Grace disappeared obediently, and we went downstairs to dinner.

CHAPTER 14

IN THE LANE

THE untroubled life, which my first calm introduction to Thornfield Hall seemed to promise, became a reality. Mrs. Fairfax remained kind and friendly. My pupil was a lively[1] child, somewhat spoilt, but she soon became obedient and willing to learn and made reasonable progress.

October, November, December, passed away. One afternoon in January, Adele was given a holiday because she had a cold. It was a fine, calm day. Mrs. Fairfax had just written a letter which was waiting to be posted, so I offered to carry it to the village, two miles away.

The ground was frozen hard; the air was still, my road was lonely. I walked fast till I got warm, then slowly, to enjoy the pleasure of the hour and the country scene. The lane[2] sloped uphill. Having walked about half-way, I sat down on a stile[3] which led to a field. From my seat I could look down on Thornfield, whose woods rose against the west. The sun went down as I watched, and I turned eastward.

On the hill-top above me sat the rising moon, pale yet as a cloud, but brightening from moment to moment. In the absolute silence I could hear plainly faint sounds of life in the distant village: I could hear, too, the flow of many little streams in the hills and valleys.

---

[1] lively = active, full of life.
[2] lane = a narrow country road.
[3] stile = a kind of step by which a person can climb over a hedge.

A loud noise broke in on these murmurings : a tramp[1], tramp
on the bridge. A horse was coming : the winding lane still
hid it, but it approached. I was just leaving the stile, but as
the path was narrow, I sat still to let the horse go by. All
sorts of fancies, bright and dark, came into my mind : the
memory of nursery stories was there among others. As this
horse approached, I remembered some of Bessie's tales of a
spirit which took the form of a horse or dog and was seen in
lonely places.

The horse was very near, but not yet in sight, when, in addition to the tramp, tramp, I heard a rush under the hedge, and a
great dog ran by, whose black-and-white coat made him a distinct object against the trees. It was a lion-like creature with
long hair and a huge head. The horse followed—a tall animal,
with a rider on its back. He passed, and I went on a few steps,
then I turned : a sliding sound, and a sudden fall, arrested
my attention. Man and horse were down ; they had slipped
on a sheet of ice. The dog came running back, and seeing
his master in difficulty, barked[2] loudly, and then ran up to
me for help. I walked down to the traveller, by this time
struggling to free himself from his horse.

" Are you hurt, sir? "

I think he was swearing : anyhow, he did not reply directly.

" Can I do anything? " I asked again.

" You must just stand to one side," he answered as he rose,
first to his knees, and then to his feet. The horse was raised,
the dog silenced. The traveller now, bending down, felt his
boot and leg, then sat down on a near-by stile.

" If you are hurt, and want help, sir, I can fetch someone
from Thornfield Hall."

" Thank you, I have no broken bones," and again he stood
up, but with an exclamation of pain.

A little daylight remained, and the moon was brightening.
I could see him plainly. He wore a riding coat with a fur
collar. He had a dark face, with stern features and a heavy

---

[1] tramp = a loud sound of heavy footsteps.
[2] bark = the noise made by an excited dog.

brow; his eyes and frowning eyebrows looked angry just now; he was past youth, but had not yet reached middle age. I felt no fear of him, and little embarrassment. Had he been a handsome-looking young gentleman, had he smiled and refused my offer gaily and with thanks, I should have gone my way, but the roughness of the traveller put me at my ease, and I remained where I was when he waved me to go, saying:

"I cannot think of leaving you, sir, at so late an hour, in this lonely spot, till I see you are fit to mount your horse."

He looked at me directly for the first time.

"I should think you ought to be at home yourself," he said. "Where do you come from?"

"From just below."

"You live just below—do you mean in that house?" pointing to Thornfield Hall.

"Yes, sir."

"Whose house is it?"

"Mr. Rochester's."

"Do you know Mr. Rochester?"

"No, I have never seen him."

"You are not a servant at the Hall, of course. You are——"
He stopped, looked at my simple dress, and seemed puzzled.

"I am the governess."

"Ah, the governess!" he repeated. "I had forgotten!"
In two minutes he rose from the stile. His face expressed pain as he tried to move.

"You may help me a little," he said, "if you will be so kind. I must beg you to come here."

I came. "Excuse me," he continued, "necessity compels me to make you useful." He laid a heavy hand on my shoulder, and leaning on me with some force, moved towards his horse. Having once caught it, he mastered it directly and sprang into his saddle.

"Now," said he, "just hand me my whip: it is over there by the hedge."

I found it.

" Thank you: now get home as fast as you can."

A touch of his heel, and horse, dog, and man had vanished down the hill.

I walked on to the village with my letter, a little stirred with excitement. It was a small event, but it marked with change one hour of my dull life.

I did not like re-entering Thornfield. To pass inside was to return to too quiet an existence. For some time I remained on the lawn. Then the clock struck, and I went in.

The hall was not dark. A warm, unaccustomed glow came from the dining-room, and through the open door I could see a bright fire. I heard a murmur of voices, and saw a group near the fireplace.

I hastened to Mrs. Fairfax's room, but I found no candle and no Mrs. Fairfax. Instead, all alone on the rug in front of her fire, I saw a large black-and-white dog. It got up and came to me. I rang the bell, for I wanted a candle. A maid entered.

" Whose dog is this? "

" He came with master."

" With whom? "

" With master—Mr. Rochester—he has just arrived."

" Indeed! Is Mrs. Fairfax with him? "

" Yes, and Miss Adele. They are in the dining-room, and John has gone for a surgeon, for master has had an accident. His horse fell."

CHAPTER 15

CONVERSATION WITH MR. ROCHESTER

FOR several days I saw little of Mr. Rochester. In the mornings he seemed much occupied with business, and in the afternoon gentlemen from the neighbourhood called and sometimes stayed to dine with him. When his foot was well enough, he rode out a good deal.

During this time, even Adele was seldom sent for to his presence, and all my acquaintance with him was limited to an

"Thank you: now get home as fast as you can."

occasional meeting about the house, when he would sometimes pass me coldly, and sometimes bow and smile. His
changes of manner did not offend me, because I saw that I
had nothing to do with the cause of them.

One day after dinner a message came that I and Adele were
to go downstairs. We descended, Adele wondering whether
the little box that she had been promised had come at last. She
was not disappointed. It stood on the dining-room table.

"My box of presents!" she exclaimed, running towards it.

"Yes, there is your box: take it into a corner and amuse
yourself," said the deep and rather scornful voice of Mr.
Rochester. "And keep quiet, do you understand."

Adele had already seized her treasure.

"Is Miss Eyre there?" the master now demanded, half
rising from his seat to look round. "Come forward, and be
seated here." He drew a chair near his own.

"I am not fond of children's talk," he continued. "Don't
draw that chair farther back; sit down exactly where I placed
it—if you please, that is. I forget these politenesses. Nor do
I care much for simple-minded old ladies. However, I must
invite mine in, I suppose."

He rang the bell for Mrs. Fairfax, and asked her to talk
to Adele.

Mr. Rochester, as he sat in his armchair, looked not quite so
stern, and much less gloomy. There was a smile on his lips,
and his eyes sparkled, probably with wine.

He had been looking for two minutes at the fire, and I had
been looking the same length of time at him, when, turning
suddenly, he caught my gaze fixed on his face.

"You examine me, Miss Eyre," he said; "do you think
me handsome?"

The answer somehow slipped from my tongue before I was
aware:

"No, sir."

"Ah! Certainly, there is something unusual about you!"
he said. "You have the appearance of a little nun[1], quiet,

[1] nun = a woman who leads a religious life away from the world.

simple, serious, yet when one asks you a question, you have a sharp answer ready. What do you mean by it? "

"Sir, I spoke too freely. I beg your pardon. I ought to have replied that tastes differ, that beauty is not important, or something of that sort."

"You ought to have replied no such thing. Beauty not important, indeed! Go on! What fault do you find with me, may I ask? "

"Mr. Rochester, I made a mistake."

"Well, you shall pay for it. Criticize me: does my forehead not please you? Now, ma'am, am I a fool? "

"Far from it, sir. You would, perhaps, think me rude if I inquired in return whether you are a kind-hearted man? "

"Another sharp answer! No, young lady, I am not—not in general; but I have a sense of duty. I once had a certain tenderness of heart, when I was young. But life has knocked me about since, and now I am hard—except, perhaps, in one or two small places. Would you say there was any hope of my losing my hardness? "

I did not know what answer to make.

"You look very much puzzled, Miss Eyre. Although you are not pretty, any more than I am handsome, a puzzled expression suits you. Besides, it is convenient, for it keeps those searching eyes of yours away from my face. Young lady, I feel conversational to-night: that is why I sent for you. It would please me now to learn more of you—therefore speak."

I sat and said nothing.

"You are dumb, Miss Eyre." He bent his head and looked at my face. "Ah! You are annoyed. Miss Eyre, I beg your pardon. I expressed myself in a stupid manner. I desire you to have the goodness to talk to me a little now."

"I am willing to amuse you, if I can, sir, but how do I know what subject will interest you? Ask me questions, and I will do my best to answer them."

"Then, in the first place, do you agree that I have the right to be a little masterful, since I am old enough to be your father, and have had a wide experience of life? "

" I don't think, sir, that you have a right to command me for such a reason. Your claim to superiority depends on the use you have made of your time."

" That would never suit my case, as I have made bad use of it. But will you still agree to receive my orders now and then, without being hurt by the tone of command? "

I smiled.

" The smile is very well," he said, catching the passing expression, " but speak too."

" I was thinking, sir, that very few masters would trouble themselves to inquire whether they hurt the feelings of those whom they paid for their services."

"'Ah! I had forgotten. I pay for your services! Well, for that reason, will you allow me to be a little commanding? "

" No, sir, not for that reason; but because you *did* forget it, and because you care about the feelings of those whom you employ, I agree willingly."

" I shake hands with you for your answer. Not three out of three thousand schoolgirl-governesses would have replied as you have done. I don't mean to praise you: if you are different from others, it is no credit to you—Nature did it. And then, I don't know you well. You may have unbearable faults as well as your few good points."

" And so may you," I thought. My eye met his as the idea passed through my mind. He seemed to read the look.

" You are right," he said, " I have plenty of faults. My past is not blameless. I was put on the wrong path when I was twenty-one, and have never got back to the right one since. I envy you your peace of mind, your clean conscience, your pure memory."

" It is never too late to mend, sir."

" What is the use of thinking of it? Since happiness is forbidden me, I have a right to get pleasure out of life."

" It will taste bitter, sir."

" Do you never laugh, Miss Eyre? Don't trouble to answer —I see you laugh rarely, yet you could be naturally merry. The Lowood discipline still remains with you, controlling your features, and you fear in the presence of a man to smile too gaily, speak too freely, or move too quickly. Yet I think you will learn to be natural with me. I see at times the look of a curious sort of bird through the close-set bars of a cage. You are going now?"

"It has struck nine, sir."

"Never mind, wait a minute: Adele is not ready to go to bed yet. I have been watching her. About ten minutes ago she pulled out of her box a little pink silk dress. joy lit up her face, and she rushed off to try it on. Soon she will return, looking exactly like her mother."

Before long, Adele's little feet were heard crossing the hall. She entered, dancing.

"Doesn't my dress look nice?" she cried, in French, "and my shoes and my stockings?"

Mr. Rochester regarded her with scorn.

"Some day I'll explain her story," he said. "Good night."

CHAPTER 16

FIRE!

MR. ROCHESTER did, on a future occasion, explain Adele's story. One afternoon I was with her in the garden, and while she played with the dog Pilot, he asked me to walk up and down a long avenue in sight of her.

He told me she was the daughter of a French dancer, whom he had once loved, but who had deceived him. She had gone away with a musician, and he had taken pity on this child whom she had left behind.

The confidence that he showed in me seemed a mark of respect, and I accepted it as such. His manner towards me had for several weeks been less changeable. He did not have moments of coldness. When he met me unexpectedly, the meeting seemed to give him pleasure: he always had a word and sometimes a smile for me: when I was summoned by formal invitation to his presence, I was honoured with a warm welcome. I, indeed, talked but little, but I enjoyed his conversation and his knowledge of the world.

His ease of manner, his friendliness, made me like him, and I felt at times as if he were my relation rather than my master. Yet he was still commanding sometimes. I did not mind this: I saw it was his way. So happy did I become with this new interest added to my life, that I no longer wished for relations, and my health improved.

And was Mr. Rochester now ugly in my eyes? No: gratitude had made his face the object that I most liked to see, and his presence in a room was more cheering than the brightest fire. I still recognized his faults, but it seemed to me that the angry look that sometimes came over his face was a remembrance of some wrong done to him in the past, and I felt sorry for him.

I was reflecting on all this one night as I prepared myself for bed. I lay down, but could not rest. I was revolving in my mind the fact that he had told me he hated Thornfield. According to Mrs. Fairfax, he seldom stayed more than two weeks at a time: yet he had now remained two months. The house would seem empty without him.

I hardly know whether I slept or not after these thoughts, but I started suddenly on hearing an indistinct murmur, peculiar and low, which sounded, I thought, just above me. I sat up in bed, listening. The sound ceased.

I tried again to sleep, but my heart beat anxiously. The clock, far down in the hall, struck two. Just then it seemed that the door of my room was touched; as if fingers had passed over the wood in feeling a way along the dark passage outside. I said: "Who is there?" Nothing answered. I grew cold with fear.

All at once I remembered it might be Pilot, who, when the kitchen door chanced to be left open, sometimes found his way up to Mr. Rochester's room. The idea calmed me somewhat, and I lay down, and as there was now an unbroken silence, I began to feel the return of sleep.

A dream was just approaching, when there was a low, deep

evil laugh, the laugh of a lost spirit, sounded, as it seemed,
at the very keyhole of my door. The sound was repeated.
My first idea was to rise and fasten the door; my next, to cry
out: "Who is there?"

Something moaned. Footsteps retreated up the passage towards the third storey staircase. A door had lately been made
to shut in that staircase; I heard it open and close.

Was that Grace Poole? It was impossible now to remain
by myself. I must go to Mrs. Fairfax. I dressed, unfastened
the door with a trembling hand, and opened it. To my surprise
there was a candle on the ground outside, and I was still more
surprised to observe that the air was quite dim, as if filled with
smoke. I became aware also of a strong smell of burning.

Something moved: it was a door left open. It was Mr
Rochester's door and the smoke rushed out from it in a cloud.
I thought no more of Mrs. Fairfax, I thought no more of Grace
Poole, or of the laugh. In an instant I was in the bedroom.
Tongues of flame flickered round the bed. The curtains were
on fire. Mr. Rochester lay stretched motionless, in a deep sleep.

"Wake up! Wake up!" I cried. I shook him, but he
only murmured and turned: the smoke had made him half
unconscious. Not a moment could be lost. I rushed to his
basin and jug. Fortunately, both were filled with water. I
lifted them with difficulty, flooded the bed and the sleeper,
flew back to my own room, brought my own water-jug, and by
God's aid succeeded in putting out the flames.

Mr. Rochester awakened at last, and I heard him using
bad language at finding himself in a pool of water.

"Is there a flood?" he asked.

"No, sir," I answered, "but there has been a fire. Get up,
do; it is out now."

"In the name of all the fairies, is that Jane Eyre?" he
demanded. "What have you done with me, witch? Did you
plan to drown me?"

"Someone has planned something: you cannot find out too
soon who and what it is."

He searched for dry clothes, and meanwhile I brought the

candle which still remained in the passage. He took it from my hand, held it up and examined the bed, all blackened and burnt, the sheets dripping, the carpet around swimming with water. I described shortly what had happened.

He listened very seriously, his face expressing more trouble than astonishment, and did not immediately speak when I had concluded.

" Shall I call Mrs. Fairfax? " I asked.

" Mrs. Fairfax? No, what would you call her for? Let her sleep in peace."

" Then I will fetch the servants."

" Not at all: just be still. Take my coat, sit down in the armchair, and keep your feet out of the wet. I am going to pay a visit to the third storey. I shall take the candle. Remain where you are: don't move, remember, or call anyone."

He went: I watched the light disappear as he moved softly along the passage. A very long time went by. I grew tired, it was cold, and I did not see the use of staying. At last he re-entered, pale and very gloomy.

" I have found it all out," he said, setting his candle down, " it is as I thought."

" How, sir? "

He made no reply, but stood looking at the ground. At the end of a few minutes, he inquired in a rather peculiar tone:

" I forget whether you said you saw anything when you opened your door."

" No, sir, only the candle outside."

" But you heard an odd laugh? You have heard that laugh before, I should think, or something like it? "

" Yes, sir: there is a woman who sews here, called Grace Poole—she laughs in that way."

" Just so, Grace Poole—you have guessed it. Well, I shall reflect on the subject. Say nothing about it: I will give some excuse for this state of affairs "—(pointing to the bed)—" and now return to your own room."

" Good night, then, sir."

" What! Are you leaving me already? "

" You said I might go, sir."

" But not without some thanks. Why, you have saved my life. At least shake hands."

He held out his hand; I gave him mine: he took it first in one, then in both his own.

" I have pleasure in owing you so immense a debt. I could not bear to owe it to anyone else in the world."

He paused and gazed at me: words trembled on his lips—but his voice was checked.

" There is no debt, sir."

" I knew," he continued, " that you would do me good in some way: I saw it in your eyes when I first met you. Their expression and smile did not "—(again he stopped)—" did not " (he went on hastily) " strike such delight in my heart for nothing. My dearest rescuer, good night! "

Strange energy was in his voice, strange fire in his look.

" I am glad I happened to be awake," I said, and then I was going.

" What! you *will* go? "

" I am cold, sir."

" Cold? Yes, and standing in a pool. Go then, Jane, go! " But he still had my hand. I thought of an excuse.

" I think I hear Mrs. Fairfax move, sir."

He loosened his fingers, and I went.

I returned to my bed, but never thought of sleep. My mind was a mixture of joy and uneasiness, judgment struggling against passion. Too feverish to rest, I rose as soon as day dawned.

CHAPTER 17

GRACE POOLE

I BOTH wished and feared to see Mr. Rochester on the day which followed this sleepless night. The morning, however, passed just as usual: nothing happened to interrupt the course of Adele's quiet studies, only soon after breakfast I heard servants busy in the neighbourhood of Mr. Rochester's bed-room. When I passed it later on I saw that all was once more in complete order. A woman was sitting on a chair by the bedside, sewing rings on to new curtains. It was Grace Poole.

There she sat, busy at her work, with her hard face and her ordinary-looking features, not in the least like a woman who had attempted murder and had been discovered. She looked up as I gazed at her, and said: " Good morning, miss," in her usual manner. No start, no change of colour betrayed emotion, consciousness of guilt, or fear of discovery.

" I will test her in some way," I thought.

" Good morning, Grace," I said aloud. " Has anything hap-pened here? I thought I heard the servants all talking together a while ago."

" Only master was reading in bed last night, and fell asleep with his candle lit, and the curtains caught fire. Fortunately, he awoke in time and put it out."

" A strange affair! " I said in a low voice, then, looking at her fixedly—" Did Mr. Rochester wake nobody? "

She raised her eyes to me, and seemed to examine me care-fully, then she answered:

" The servants sleep so far off, you know, miss, that they would not be likely to hear. Mrs. Fairfax's room and yours are nearest to master's. Mrs. Fairfax says she heard nothing: when people are getting old they often sleep heavily." She paused, and then added, with an appearance of carelessness— " But you are young, miss, and perhaps a light sleeper. Did you hear a noise? "

" I did," I said in a low voice, " and at first I thought it was Pilot, but Pilot cannot laugh, and I am certain I heard a laugh, and a strange one."

She threaded her needle with a steady hand, and then ob-served calmly:

" It is hardly likely that master would laugh, miss, when he was in danger. You must have been dreaming."

" I was not dreaming," I replied. Again she looked at me.

"Have you told master that you heard a laugh?" she inquired.

"I have not had the opportunity of speaking to him this morning."

"You did not think of opening your door, and looking out?"

"Quite the opposite," I said. "I bolted my door."

"Then you are not in the habit of bolting your door every night?"

The idea occurred to me that if she discovered that I knew or suspected her guilt, she would be playing some of her evil tricks on me. Perhaps she was trying to find out my habits. I replied sharply:

"In future I shall take good care to fasten everything before I lie down."

"It would be wise to do so," was her answer.

I hardly heard Mrs. Fairfax's account of the fire during dinner. I was occupied in puzzling my brains over the mysterious character of Grace Poole, and still more over her position at Thornfield, and the reason why she had not been arrested, or at least dismissed from service. Mr. Rochester had admitted her guilt, but had made me swear to keep it secret. It was strange that a bold, proud gentleman should be in the power of one of his own servants.

I waited impatiently for the hour when I should see Mr. Rochester that evening. I had so many things to say to him. I wanted to introduce the subject of Grace Poole, and hear what he would answer.

At last a servant made her appearance, but it was only to say that tea was ready in Mrs. Fairfax's room.

"You must want your tea," said the good lady, as I joined her, "you ate so little at dinner. I am afraid you are not well to-day: you look feverish."

"Oh, I am quite well!"

"Mr. Rochester has had a favourable day for his journey," she went on.

"Journey! Has Mr. Rochester gone anywhere?"

" Oh, he set out the moment he had breakfasted. He has gone to the Leas, Mr. Eshton's house, ten miles on the other side of Millcote. I believe there is quite a party assembled there."

" Do you expect him back to-night? "

" No; I should think he is very likely to stay a week or more. Mr. Rochester is so accomplished and lively in society that I believe he is popular everywhere. The ladies are very fond of him."

" Are there ladies at the Leas? "

" There are Mrs. Eshton and her daughters—very fashionable young ladies indeed: and there are the Misses Blanche and Mary Ingram, most beautiful women. When Blanche was here at a Christmas entertainment, she was considered the beauty of the evening."

" What was she like? "

" Tall, with a long, graceful neck, noble features, large black eyes, as bright as her jewels, and a fine head of black curly hair."

" She was greatly admired, of course? "

" Yes, and not only for her beauty, but for her accomplishments. She sings. She and Mr. Rochester sang together."

" I was not aware that Mr. Rochester could sing."

" Oh, he has a fine voice, and an excellent taste in music. He thinks very highly of Miss Ingram's singing."

" And this beautiful and accomplished lady is not yet married? "

" I believe that neither she nor her sister have very large fortunes."

When I was once more alone, I reviewed the information that I had received. I looked into my heart, examined its thoughts and feelings, and tried to bring them back to common sense. I addressed myself with severity:

" A greater fool than you, Jane Eyre, never breathed the breath of life. *You* favoured by Mr. Rochester? *You* of importance to him in any way? Go! your foolishness disgusts me. The attentions paid to a woman by her superior mean nothing to him. It is madness to let a secret love take fire within one.

"Listen then, Jane Eyre, to your punishment. To-morrow, place the looking-glass before you, and draw yourself faithfully, without softening one fault. Write under it: 'Picture of a Governess, poor and plain.'

"Afterwards, draw the loveliest face that you can imagine, paint it in your softest colours, according to the description given by Mrs. Fairfax. Call it ' Blanche, an accomplished lady of rank.'

"Whenever, in future, you should chance to suppose that Mr. Rochester thinks well of you, take out the two pictures and compare them."

I did so, and before long I had cause to congratulate myself on the discipline to which I had forced my feelings to submit.

CHAPTER 18

HOUSE-PARTY

MR. ROCHESTER had been absent more than two weeks, when Mrs. Fairfax received a letter from him.

While she broke the seal and read, I went on taking my coffee. My hand shook, and I spilt half the contents of my cup into my saucer.

"Well, I sometimes think we are too quiet, but now we are to be busy enough for a little while at least," she declared. "Mr. Rochester will be here in three days' time, and a great many fine people are coming with him. He sends instructions for the whole house to be prepared." Mrs. Fairfax finished her breakfast and hastened away to begin operations.

The next three days were busy enough. I never saw such washing, brushing, beating of carpets, polishing of glasses, taking down and putting up of pictures. Adele ran quite wild in the midst of it, dancing about the house, and looking over her dresses. She was excused from school duties. Mrs. Fairfax asked for my help, and I was all day in the storeroom assisting her and the cook. I had no time for dark thoughts, and I was as active and gay as anyone. Then I chanced to see the third storey staircase door open and Grace Poole descend, as was her custom, to eat her dinner in the kitchen, and I received a check to my cheerfulness.

The strangest thing of all was that no one in the house, except me, seemed to notice her habits, or wonder about them. No one discussed her position or employment. I did, indeed, once by accident hear part of a conversation on the subject between two of the servants.

"She gets good wages, I suppose?"

"Yes, I wish I had as good: not that I complain of mine, but they're not one fifth of the sum Mrs. Poole receives."

"She's good at her work, I expect."

"Ah! She understands what she has to do. Not everyone could do her job."

"That's true! I wonder whether the master . . ."

At that moment one of them noticed me, and made a sign to her companion to be careful.

"Doesn't she know?" I heard the latter whisper.

The first one shook her head, and they both became silent.

The three days passed, and on the afternoon of the fourth day Mrs. Fairfax dressed herself in her best black silk dress, and put on her gold watch, for it was her business to receive the company, show the ladies to their rooms, and so on.

At last wheels were heard. Four riders came swiftly up the avenue, followed by two carriages. Two of the riders were young gentlemen, the third was Mr. Rochester, and the fourth, who rode by his side, was a lady.

"Miss Ingram!" exclaimed Mrs. Fairfax, and she hurried away to her post below.

A joyful stir was now heard in the hall: gentlemen's deep tones and ladies' silvery voices sounded together; clear above all, though not so loud, was the voice of the master of Thornfield Hall welcoming his guests.

Adele begged to go down, and I had difficulty in making her

understand that in no circumstances must she do so unless sent for. I told her stories as long as she would listen to them, then for a change took her out to look down the stairs and watch the servants passing backwards and forwards with a meal. When the evening was far advanced, there was a sound of music from the drawing-room, followed by conversation. I listened long. Suddenly I discovered that I was trying to catch the voice of my master, and to understand what he was saying.

The next day, Mrs. Fairfax said to me:

" I happened to remark to Mr. Rochester how much Adele wished to be introduced to the ladies, and he said: ' Oh, let her come to the drawing-room after dinner, and request Miss Eyre to accompany her.' "

" He said that from mere politeness; I need not go, I am sure."

" Well, I remarked to him that you were unused to society and would not like appearing in so gay a gathering, and he replied, in his quick way: ' Nonsense! If she objects, tell her it is my particular wish; and if she resists, say that I shall come and fetch her.' "

" I will not give him that trouble. Will you be there, Mrs. Fairfax? "

" No, I begged to be excused. I'll tell you how to avoid the embarrassment of a formal entrance. You must go into the drawing-room while it is empty, before the ladies leave the dinner-table. Choose your seat in any quiet corner. You need not stay long after the gentlemen come in: just let Mr. Rochester see that you are there, and then slip away. Nobody will notice you."

CHAPTER 19

IN THE DRAWING-ROOM

I FELT rather nervous as the hour approached when I was to appear in the drawing-room. Adele had been in a state of joy all day, but when the operation of dressing began, she became serious. I myself quickly put on my best dress (a silver-grey one, bought for Miss Temple's wedding and never worn since) and smoothed my hair.

We found the room empty. A large fire was burning, and wax candles shone among the lovely flowers on the tables.

Adele brought a small chair to my side. Before long she touched my knee.

" May I take one of these beautiful flowers—just as a finishing touch to my dress! "

" You think too much of your dress, Adele: but you may have a flower." And I took a rose and fastened it in her belt. She sighed with satisfaction, and I turned away to hide a smile.

A soft sound of rising could now be heard. The curtain across the arch that divided the two rooms was drawn aside, and a number of ladies entered. I rose and bowed to them. One or two bent their heads in return, the others only stared at me.

They scattered about the room like a flock of birds, looking at the books and flowers and talking in low but clear tones. I examined them quietly, giving most of my attention to the Ingrams. The mother, Lady Ingram, was a splendidly handsome woman, but with an expression of almost unbearable pride and a fierce, hard eye that reminded me of Mrs. Reed. The daughters, Blanche and Mary, were both very tall. I looked with special interest, of course, at the elder. How far was she like Mrs. Fairfax's description, and the picture called up by my own imagination?

She was beautiful, but her face was like her mother's, only younger. She was talking to Mrs. Dent, a gentle lady, in such a way as to show her own cleverness but make the latter appear ignorant.

Meanwhile Adele advanced and greeted the company in French. Miss Ingram looked down on her mockingly. Mrs. Dent kissed her kindly, and Amy and Louisa Eshton seated her on a couch between them and were spoiling her as much as she could wish.

At last coffee was brought in, and the gentlemen were summoned. I sat in the shadow: the window-curtain half hid me.

Mr. Rochester came in last: I was not looking, yet I saw him enter. I tried to keep my attention on my sewing. I remembered the last time I saw him, and how near I had approached him at that moment. Yet now, how distant, how far apart we were! He took a seat at the other side of the room without looking at me.

Against my will my eyes were drawn to his face. I compared him with his guests; he was not beautiful. But his colourless face, square, heavy brow, broad black eyebrows, deep eyes, firm mouth—all energy, decision, will—were full of interest to me. I had not intended to love him, but the first time I saw him again, my feelings overcame me. He made me love him without looking at me.

I saw Mr. Rochester smile. He was talking at the moment to Louisa and Amy Eshton. I saw with surprise that they received that look calmly, yet I was glad. " He is not to them what he is to me," I thought: " he is not of their kind. I believe he is of mine. Though rank and wealth separate us widely, I have something in my brain and heart in common with him. I have certain tastes and feelings that he understands."

Coffee was handed round. The ladies had become gay since the gentlemen entered. The older men argued about politics while their wives listened. All were occupied except Blanche Ingram, who stood alone at the table. She moved towards Mr. Rochester.

" Mr. Rochester, why did you take charge of a little thing like that? "—(pointing to Adele)—" where did you get her from? "

" She was left on my hands."

" You should have sent her to school."

" I could not afford it. Schools are so dear."

" Why, I suppose you have a governess for her: I saw a person with her just now—has she gone? Oh, no! there she is still, behind the window-curtain. You pay her, of course. I should think it quite as expensive—more so; for you have to maintain them both in addition."

" I have not considered the subject."

"No, you men never do consider saving. You should hear mama speak on the subject of governesses. Mary and I had, I should think, half a dozen at least; half of them we hated, the rest we laughed at. They were all nuisances—were they not, mama?"

"My dearest, don't mention governesses; the word upsets me. I have suffered so much from their stupidity. I thank heaven I have done with them."

Mrs. Dent here bent over and whispered something in her ear, reminding the lady, I suppose, that one of the cursed profession was present.

"Let her listen!" said her ladyship, "I hope it may do her good!" Then, in a lower tone, but still loud enough for me to hear, "I noticed her, and I see in her face all the faults of her kind."

"Oh, mama! Do not weary us with the description. Let us change the subject. How is your voice to-night, Mr. Rochester?"

"At your service, if you command it."

Miss Ingram seated herself with proud grace at the piano.

"Mr. Rochester, now sing, and I will play for you."

"I am all obedience."

"Now is my time to slip away," I thought, but the voice that began to sing arrested my attention. It was a fine, powerful one, into which the singer threw his own feelings. I waited till the last notes died away, and then slipped out by the side door. In crossing the hall, I noticed that my shoe was undone. I stopped to tie it.

I heard the drawing-room door open; a gentleman came out. Rising hastily, I stood face to face with him. It was Mr. Rochester.

"How do you do?" he said.

"I am very well, sir."

"Why did you not come and speak to me in the room?"

I thought I might have put the same question, but I would not speak so freely. I answered:

"I did not wish to disturb you, as you seemed occupied."

" What have you been doing during my absence? "

" Nothing particular; teaching Adele as usual."

" And getting a good deal paler than you were. What is the matter? "

" Nothing at all, sir."

" Did you catch a cold that night when you half drowned me? "

" No."

" Return to the drawing-room: you are deserting too early."

" I am tired, sir."

He looked at me for a minute.

" And a little unhappy. What about? Tell me."

" Nothing—nothing, sir. I am not unhappy."

" But you are—so much so that a few more words would bring tears to your eyes. Indeed, they are there now. If I had the time, I would know what this all means. Well, to-night I excuse you, but as long as my visitors stay, I expect you to appear in the drawing-room every evening. Now go, and send the nurse for Adele. Good night, my——" He stopped, bit his lip, and quickly left me.

CHAPTER 20

FORTUNE-TELLING

THOSE were merry days at Thornfield Hall, and busy days too: how different from the first three months of uneventful stillness I had passed beneath its roof! There was life everywhere, movement all day long. The drawing-rooms were only quiet when the fine spring weather called the guests out into the garden.

Even when rain fell for some days, no shadow seemed cast over their enjoyment. Indoor amusements only became more lively and varied.

One day Mr. Rochester was summoned to Millcote on business. The afternoon was wet, and the guests did not seem to know how to occupy themselves, for if he was absent even an hour, they seemed to lose their gaiety.

Some of the younger ladies and gentlemen began to talk idly. The older ones settled down to a quiet game of cards. Blanche Ingram repelled the efforts made to draw her into the conversation, and first played over some tunes idly on the piano; then, having fetched a novel from the library, she sank down in an armchair to pass the time reading.

It was nearly time to dress for dinner, when little Adele, who was kneeling by me on the drawing-room window-seat, suddenly exclaimed:

"There's Mr. Rochester coming back."

I turned, and Miss Ingram rushed forward, for at the same time a sound of wheels and a noise of horses' feet could be heard.

"Why is he coming home in a carriage?" said Miss Ingram. "He went out on horseback, did he not?"

As she said this, a gentleman descended from the carriage in travelling dress—a stranger.

"How annoying!" exclaimed Miss Ingram: "you trouble-some monkey!"—(addressing Adele)—"who put you up there in the window to give false information?" and she gave me an angry look, as if I were to blame.

Some conversation could be heard in the hall, and soon the newcomer entered. He bowed to Lady Ingram, judging her the eldest lady present.

"It appears I come at an awkward time, madam," he said, "when my friend, Mr. Rochester, is away from home; but I have had a very long journey, and I think I may take the liberty of remaining here till he returns."

I soon learned that his name was Mason, and that he had only recently arrived from the West Indies, where he first met Mr. Rochester. His manner was polite, his pronunciation a little unusual. His features were regular, but his eye wandered, and his expression was both unsettled and lacking in life. For my master he seemed an odd kind of friend.

I was reflecting on this, when something unexpected happened. Mr. Mason, not being used to cold weather, asked for more coal to be put on the fire. The servant who brought it stopped near Mr. Eshton's chair and said something to him in a low voice.

"Tell her she shall be punished if she does not take herself away," replied the gentleman.

"No . . . stop!" interrupted Colonel Dent. "Don't send her away, Eshton: she might amuse the ladies." And speaking aloud, he continued: "Ladies, there is an old woman in the servants' hall who insists upon being brought in to tell our fortunes.[1] Would you like to see her?"

"Surely, Colonel," cried Lady Ingram, "you would not encourage such a deceiver? Dismiss her, by all means, at once!"

"But I cannot persuade her to go away, my lady," said the servant. "She says she will not move until she gets permission to come in here."

"What is she like?" inquired the Misses Eshton, together.

"A shockingly ugly old creature, miss, almost as black as coal."

"Why, she's a real witch[2]," cried one of the young men. "Let us have her in, of course."

"My dear boy, what are you thinking about?" exclaimed his mother.

"I cannot possibly allow such a thing," added Lady Ingram.

"Indeed, mama, but you can—and will," pronounced the voice of Blanche, as she turned round on the piano-seat. "I have a curiosity to hear my fortune told: therefore, bring the old woman in."

"My dearest Blanche! Reflect . . ."

"I do: and I must have her . . . quick!"

The servant still hesitated.

"She looks such a rough one," he said.

"Go!" exclaimed Miss Ingram, and the man went. A minute later he returned.

---

[1] tell one's fortune = prophesy one's future, usually by examining one's hand.

[2] witch = a woman with magic powers.

"She won't come now," he said. "She says I must take her into a room by herself, and then those who wish to consult her must go to her one by one."

"You see now," began Lady Ingram, "she takes advantage. Be advised, my angel——"

"Show her into the library, of course," interrupted her daughter.

"I think I had better just look at her before any of the ladies go," said Colonel Dent.

The servant went and returned once more.

"She says, sir, that she'll have no gentlemen, nor any ladies," he added, keeping a straight face,[1] with difficulty, "except the young and unmarried."

Miss Ingram rose solemnly. "I go first," she said.

"Oh, my best! oh, my dearest! pause . . . reflect!" was her mother's cry, but Blanche passed out of the room without a word.

A silence followed. Lady Ingram looked despairing. Miss Mary declared that she could never venture. Amy and Louisa Eshton laughed nervously and appeared a little frightened.

The minutes passed very slowly: fifteen were counted before the library door again opened, and Miss Ingram returned to us.

Would she laugh? Would she take it as a joke? All eyes met hers with a glance of eager curiosity. She walked stiffly to her seat and took it.

"Well, Blanche?"

"What did she say?"

"Now, now, good people," replied Miss Ingram, "don't get so excited. I have seen an old woman, who has told me what fortune-tellers usually tell. My fancy has been satisfied, and that's all."

She took up a book, leant back in her chair, and refused further conversation. For half an hour she never turned a page, and her face grew darker and more dissatisfied.

Meanwhile Mary Ingram, and Amy and Louisa Eshton, declared they dared not go alone; and yet they all wished to

---

[1] keep a straight face = keep oneself from smiling.

go. After the exchange of many messages through the servant, permission was at last given for the three of them to go together.

Their visit was not so quiet as Miss Ingram's had been. We heard nervous laughter and little cries from the library, and after about twenty minutes they burst into the room running and half frightened.

" I am sure she has strange powers! " they cried. " She told us such things! She knows all about us! " and they sank breathless in the various seats the gentlemen hastened to bring them.

Urged for further explanation, they declared that she told them of things which they had said and done in their childhood, and described possessions that they had at home. She had even guessed their thoughts, and whispered in the ear of each the name of the person she liked best in the world.

Here the gentlemen begged earnestly to be given more information on the last point, but they only got blushes and laughter in return. The elder ladies tried to calm the younger, while their husbands laughed.

As I watched this scene, I heard a voice at my elbow. I turned and saw the servant.

" If you please, miss, the old woman declares there is another unmarried young lady in the room, and swears she will not go till she has seen all. What shall I tell her? "

" Oh, I will go, certainly," I answered. I was glad of the opportunity to satisfy my curiosity. I slipped out of the room unnoticed and closed the door quietly behind me.

CHAPTER 21

THE FORTUNE-TELLER

THE library looked quiet enough as I entered it, and the witch —if she really were such—was seated in an armchair by the fire. She had a loose red garment wrapped around her and a wide hat tied down with a handkerchief under her chin. She seemed to be reading from a little black book, and murmured the words to herself, as most old women do, while she read.

As I stood on the rug and warmed my hands, I felt as calm as ever I did in my life. The woman shut her book and looked up slowly; her hat partly shaded her face, but I could see that it was a strange one, and that she had a great deal of untidy hair. Her eyes met mine with a bold and direct gaze.

"Well, and you want your fortune told?" she said in a voice as rough as her appearance.

"I don't care about it, mother; you may please yourself: but I ought to warn you, I shall not believe you."

"It's the sort of answer I expected of you. I heard it in your step as you came in."

"Did you? You've a quick ear."

"I have; and a quick eye and a quick brain. I need them; especially when I've people like you to deal with. Why don't you tremble?"

"I'm not cold."

"Why don't you turn pale?"

"I am not sick."

"Why don't you consult me about your future?"

"I'm not silly."

The old woman gave a high thin-sounding laugh, and lighting a short black pipe, began to smoke. After several minutes she raised her bent body, took the pipe from her lips, and said:

"You are cold; you are sick; and you are silly."

"Prove it," I returned.

"You are cold, because you are alone. Nothing strikes the fire from you that is in you. You are sick, because the best of feelings, the highest and sweetest given to man, keeps away from you. You are silly, because however much you suffer, you will make no sign to it to approach, nor will you stir one step to meet it where it waits you."

"You might say that to almost anyone living in my circumstances."

"There is scarcely anyone living in just your circumstances. If you knew it, you are peculiarly situated: very near happiness; yes, within reach of it. The materials are all prepared; only a movement is needed to combine them."

"I don't understand mysteries."

"If you wish me to speak more plainly, show me your hand."

"And I must cross it with silver,[1] I suppose?"

"Of course."

I gave her a shilling. She put it in an old stocking, tied it up, and approached her face to my hand.

"It is too fine," she said. "I cannot read it. Besides, fate is not written in a hand. It is in the face. Kneel, and lift up your head."

"Ah! now you are coming to reality," I said, as I obeyed her.

She stirred the fire so that a flicker of light broke from the disturbed coal and fell full upon me.

"I wonder what thoughts are busy in your heart during all the hours you sit among the fine people yonder," she said, when she had examined me a while.

"I feel tired often, sleepy sometimes, but seldom sad."

"Then you have some secret hope to support you and please you with whispers of the future?"

"Not I. The most I hope is to save enough money to set up a little school of my own some day."

"A poor food for the spirit to exist on: and, sitting in that window-seat (you see I know your habits) . . ."

"You have learnt them from the servants."

"Ah! You think yourself sharp. Well, to tell the truth, I am acquainted with one of them, Mrs. Poole . . ."

I started to my feet.

"You are . . . are you?" I thought; "there is something queer about this."

"Don't be alarmed," continued the strange creature. "You

[1] cross one's hand with silver = pay money (in fortune-tellers' language only).

can trust **Mrs. Poole**, she can keep a secret. But as I was saying: sitting in that window-seat, do you think of nothing but your future school? Is there not one face that you study? Or maybe two? "

" I like to study all the faces."

" But when a lady, young and beautiful and of high rank, sits and smiles in the eyes of a gentleman whom you . . ."

" Whom what? "

" Whom you know . . . and perhaps think well of him."

" I don't know the gentlemen here. I have scarcely spoken a word to any of them."

" Will you say that of the master of the house! "

" He is not at home."

" And because he is away from here for a few hours, do you then deny his acquaintance? "

" No, but I do not see what Mr. Rochester has to do with the subject."

" I was talking of ladies smiling into the eyes of gentlemen."

" Mr. Rochester has a right to enjoy the society of his guests."

" Yes, Mr. Rochester has sat for hours, his ear towards those charming lips, looking grateful for the entertainment given him."

" Grateful! I cannot remember observing gratitude in his face."

" Observing! You have watched him closely, then. What did you observe, if not gratitude? You have seen love, have you not? . . . and, looking into the future, you have seen him married, and his bride happy? "

" Not exactly. Your witch's skill is at fault sometimes."

" What in the world have you seen, then? "

" Never mind: I came here to inquire, not to confess. Is it known that Mr. Rochester is to be married? "

" Yes; and to the beautiful Miss Ingram. He must love such a fair lady; and probably she loves him, or at least his purse. Yet I told her something about the Rochester property half an hour ago, that made her look rather anxious."

"But, mother, you have told me nothing of my own fortune."

"Yours is as yet doubtful: when I examined your face, one feature promised one thing, another the opposite. Chance has laid on one side a measure of happiness for you. It depends on yourself to stretch out your hand and take it up: but whether you will do so, is the problem I study. Kneel again on the rug."

"Don't keep me long; the fire burns me."

"The flame flickers in the eye; the eye shines like dew; it looks soft and full of feeling; it smiles at my words. it is open to influence. When it ceases to smile, it is sad: it shows heaviness of spirit resulting from loneliness. It turns from me with a mocking look; it seems to deny the truth of my discoveries. Its pride and restraint only strengthen me in my opinion. The eye is favourable.

"As to the mouth, it delights at times in laughter; it tends to express its owner's thoughts, but it may be silent about her feelings. It is a mouth that requires human affection. That too is favourable.

"I can see no enemy but in the forehead, and that forehead seems to say: 'I can live alone, if self-respect and circumstances require me to do so.' Reason sits firm and will not let the feelings burst forth. The passions may rage and the desires imagine all sorts of vain things, but judgment shall conquer in every argument.

"Well said, forehead; your declaration shall be respected. I have formed my plans, and in them I have attended to the claims of conscience. My harvest must be smiles, not tears. But I have said enough. So far I have kept myself under control, but further might try me beyond my strength. Rise, Miss Eyre: leave me; the play is over."

Where was I? Did I wake or sleep? The old woman's voice had changed: it was now familiar to me as my own face in a glass. I got up, but did not go. The witch again made a sign to me to depart. The fire shone on her arm: it was round, not withered; a broad ring flashed on the little finger: I had seen it many times before.

"Well, Jane, do you know me?" asked the familiar voice.

"Only take off these red rags, sir, and then . . ."

"But the string is in a knot . . . help me."

"Break it, sir."

"There, then . . ." And Mr. Rochester stepped out of his borrowed garments.

"Now, sir, what a strange idea!"

"But well carried out, eh? Don't you think so?"

"With the ladies you must have managed well."

"But not with you?"

"You did not act the character of a witch with me."

"What character did I act? My own?"

"No. I believe you have been trying to make me speak too freely; you have been talking nonsense to make me talk nonsense. It is scarcely fair, sir."

"Do you forgive me, Jane?"

"I cannot tell till I have thought about it. If, on reflection, I find I have said nothing very foolish, I shall try to forgive you; but it was not right."

"Oh, you have been very correct—very careful, very sensible."

I reflected, and thought, on the whole, I had. It was a comfort; but, indeed, I had been suspicious almost from the beginning of the interview. I knew that fortune-tellers did not express themselves like this seeming old woman. My mind, however, had been full of Grace Poole. I had never thought of Mr. Rochester.

"Well," he said, "what are you thinking about? What does that calm smile mean?"

"Wonder and self-congratulation, sir. I have your permission to go now, I suppose?"

"No, stay a moment."

"I had better not remain long, sir; it must be near eleven o'clock. Oh, are you aware, Mr. Rochester, that a stranger has arrived here since you left this morning?"

"A stranger! I expected no one; has he gone?"

"No, he said he had known you a long time. His name is

Mason, and he comes from the West Indies; from Spanish Town, in Jamaica, I think."

Mr. Rochester was standing near me; he had taken my hand, as if to lead me to a chair. As I spoke he grasped my wrist violently; the smile on his lips froze, and he breathed quickly. He repeated the words "Mason . . . the West Indies!" several times, growing as he spoke whiter than ashes: he hardly seemed to know what he was doing.

"Do you feel ill, sir?" I inquired.

"Jane, I've had a blow; I've had a blow, Jane!" He staggered.

"Oh, lean on me, sir."

"Jane, you offered me your shoulder once before; let me have it now."

He sat down, and made me sit beside him.

"My little friend!" he said, "I wish I were on a quiet island alone with you; and with trouble, and danger, and evil memories removed from me."

"Can I help you, sir?"

"Fetch me, Jane, a glass of wine from the dining-room."

I went. I found all the party at supper. I filled a wine-glass (I saw Miss Ingram watch me frowningly as I did so: she thought I was taking it for myself) and returned.

Mr. Rochester's extreme paleness had disappeared, and he looked once more firm and stern. He took the glass from my hand, swallowed the contents, and gave it back to me.

"What are they doing, Jane?"

"Laughing and talking, sir."

"They don't look solemn and mysterious, as if they had heard something strange?"

"Not at all, they are full of gaiety."

"And Mason?"

"He was laughing too."

"If all these people turned away from me in scorn, what would you do, Jane? Would you go with them?"

"I rather think not, sir. I should have more pleasure in staying with you."

"And if they cast you out from society for supporting me?"

"I could bear that for the sake of any friend who deserves my support; as you do, I am sure."

"Go back now into the dining-room; step quietly up to Mason, and whisper in his ear that Mr. Rochester has come and wishes to see him: bring him in here and then leave me."

"Yes, sir."

I obeyed. All the company stared at me as I passed straight among them. I went up to Mr. Mason, and did as I had been instructed.

At a late hour, after I had been in bed some time, I heard Mr. Rochester's voice say:

"This way, Mason: this is your room. Good night."

He spoke cheerfully: the gay tones set my heart at rest. I was soon asleep.

CHAPTER 22

A CRY IN THE NIGHT

I HAD forgotten to draw my curtain, and when the moon, which was full and bright, came and looked at me through the window, I opened my eyes. I half rose, and raised my arm to shut out the light.

Good God! What a cry!

The night—its silence—its rest, was torn by a wild sharp sound that ran from end to end of Thornfield Hall.

My heart stood still: my outstretched arm remained motionless. The cry died away.

It came from the third storey, above me. And above me —yes, in the room just over my head—I now heard a struggle: a deadly one it seemed from the noise; and a breathless voice shouted:

"Help! help! help!" and then: "Rochester! for God's sake, come!"

A door opened: someone ran, or rushed, along the passage. Above me something fell, and there was silence.

I put on some clothes, though my limbs shook with horror, and ventured outside. Door after door opened: the guests were all aroused: exclamations, terrified murmurs, sounded everywhere. " Oh, what is it? "—" Who was hurt? "—" What has happened? "—" Are there robbers? " was demanded on all sides.

" Where is Rochester? " cried Colonel Dent. " I cannot find him in his bed."

" Here! Here! " was shouted in return. " Be calm, all of you: I'm coming."

The door at the end of the passage opened, and Mr. Rochester advanced with a candle: he had descended from the third storey. One of the ladies ran to him directly; she seized his arm: it was Miss Ingram. The Misses Eshton followed.

" All's well! All's well! " he cried. " It's a mere nothing. Ladies, keep off, or I shall become dangerous."

And he looked dangerous: his black eyes flashed. Calming himself with an effort he added:

" A servant has had a bad dream: that is all. She's a nervous person, easily excited: she imagined she saw a ghost, and has been taken ill with fright. Now, I must see you all back into your rooms, for, till the house is settled, she cannot be looked after."

So, by persuasion and command, he succeeded in getting them to return to rest. I retreated unnoticed to my room— but I did not go to bed. Instead, I began to dress myself carefully. The sounds I had heard after the scream, and the words that had been spoken, assured me that it was not a servant's dream that had thus aroused the house, and that the explanation that Mr. Rochester had given was merely an invention to calm his guests. I dressed, so as to be ready if needed, and sat a long time by the window.

Stillness returned: each murmur and movement ceased gradually, and in about an hour Thornfield Hall seemed once again asleep. The moon was about to set, and I thought I would lie down again, dressed as I was. As I bent to take off my shoes, a cautious hand tapped at the door.

" Are you up? " asked the voice that I expected to hear.

" Yes, sir."

" And dressed? "

" Yes."

" Come out, then, quietly."

I obeyed. Mr. Rochester stood in the passage holding a light.

" I want you," he said, " come this way. Don't hurry, and don't make a noise."

He moved silently along the passage and up the stairs, to the third storey. I followed. He held a key in his hand, and approaching one of the small doors, put it in the lock. He paused.

" You don't turn sick at the sight of blood? "

" I think I shall not, but I have never been tested."

He turned the key and opened the door. I saw a room that I remembered to have seen before, the day that Mrs. Fairfax showed me over the house, but now an inner door was visible, which had been hidden then behind a curtain. This door was open, and I heard from the room beyond a wild, animal-like sound, almost like dogs quarrelling. Mr. Rochester, putting down his candle, said to me: " Wait a minute," and went forward to the inner room. A shout of laughter greeted his entrance, noisy at first, and ending in Grace Poole's ghostly: " Ha! ha! " *She*, then, was there.

In a moment my master came out and closed the door.

" Here, Jane," he said, and I walked round a screen to the other side of a large bed, with curtains drawn around it. An armchair was near the bed, and a man sat in it, dressed except for his coat. I recognized his pale and seemingly lifeless face —the stranger, Mason. I saw, too, that his shirt on one side and one arm, was dripping with blood.

" Hold the candle," said Mr. Rochester. I took it. He fetched a basin of water, opened the shirt of the wounded

"Hold the candle," said Mr. Rochester.

man, and began to wash away the blood, which was flowing fast. Mr. Mason soon opened his eyes and moaned.

" Is there immediate danger? " he asked.

" No—it's a mere scratch. Don't be overcome, man! I'll fetch a surgeon for you now, myself. You'll be able to be removed by morning. Jane," he continued.

" Sir? "

" I shall have to leave you in this room with this gentleman for an hour, or perhaps two hours. You will wash away the blood when it returns. If he feels faint you will put a glass of water to his lips. You will not speak to him at all—and Richard, it will be at the risk of your life if you speak to her: if you excite yourself, I cannot be responsible for what may happen."

Again the poor man moaned. Mr. Rochester watched me carry on his task for a moment. Then, saying, " Remember! —no conversation," he left the room. I experienced a strange feeling as the key turned in the lock, and the sound of his retreating step ceased to be heard.

Here I was in the third storey, fastened into one of its rooms, a pale and bloody spectacle under my eyes, a murderess hardly separated from me by a single door. The rest I could bear, but I trembled at the thought of Grace Poole bursting out upon me.

I must keep to my post, however. And I had to listen as well as to watch. I listened—but all night I heard only three sounds—a footstep, an animal murmur, and a deep human moan.

My own thoughts, too, worried me. What crime was this, what mystery, that broke out now in fire and now in blood, at the dead of night? What creature was it, that in an ordinary woman's shape, possessed the voice, now of a mocking spirit, and now of a wild animal? And this man I now bent over, this quiet stranger—how had he become mixed up in this affair of horror? What made him seek this part of the house? Why did he submit to Mr. Rochester's demands for secrecy? Why did Mr. Rochester enforce this secrecy?

" When will he come? When will he come? " I cried to

myself, as the night slowly passed, as my bleeding patient moaned, and no aid came.

CHAPTER 23

DAWN

THE candle at last went out, and a grey light outside the window showed that dawn was approaching. Presently I heard the dog bark far below. Hope returned.

Five minutes later, Mr. Rochester entered, and with him the surgeon he had been to fetch.

"Now, Carter, be quick," he said to the latter. "I give you only half an hour for attending to the wound, fastening the bandages, getting the patient downstairs and all."

"But is he fit to move, sir?"

"Yes, yes; it is nothing serious: he is upset, he needs encouragement. Come, set to work."

He approached Mason.

"Now, my good fellow, how are you?" he asked.

"She's finished me, I fear," was the faint reply.

"Courage! You've lost a little blood, that's all. Carter, assure him there's no danger."

"I can do that conscientiously," said the surgeon; "only I wish I could have got here sooner. But how is this? This wound on the shoulder was not done with a knife: there have been teeth here!"

"She bit me," murmured Mason. "She attacked me like a tigress, when Rochester got the knife from her. I did not expect it: she looked so quiet at first."

"I warned you," was his friend's answer. "I told you to be careful when you went near her. Besides, you might have waited till to-morrow, and had me with you."

"I thought I could have done some good."

"You thought! you thought! Yes, it makes me impatient to hear you. However, you have suffered for not taking my advice. Carter, hurry! hurry! The sun will soon rise, and I must have him away from here."

"Directly, sir; but I must look at this other wound in the arm: she has had her teeth here, too, I think."

"She sucked the blood: she said she'd empty my heart," said Mason.

I saw a peculiarly strong expression of disgust, horror, hatred, pass across Mr. Rochester's face, but he only said:

"Come, be silent, Richard, and never mind her nonsense: don't repeat it. Jane," he continued, turning to me. "Take this key: go down to my bedroom, and bring a clean shirt. Then go into Mr. Mason's room and find his coat."

I obeyed. In a short time the wounded man was dressed and lifted to his feet. It was by this time half-past five. Supported by Mr. Rochester and the surgeon, he seemed to walk fairly easily, and was got downstairs with as little noise as possible. Outside a carriage was waiting.

"Take care of him," said Mr. Rochester, as Carter followed Mason into the carriage, "and keep him at your house till he is quite well. Good-bye, Richard."

"Rochester . . ."

"What is it?"

"Let her be taken care of; let her be treated tenderly; let her . . ." he stopped and burst into tears.

"I do my best, and have done it, and will do it," was the answer. Mr. Rochester shut the door, and the carriage drove away.

"I wish God would put an end to all this!" he added.

He moved with slow step towards a door in the wall bordering the fruit garden. He opened it, and stood waiting for me.

"Jane," he said, "come where there is some freshness, for a few moments. That house is a mere prison, don't you feel it so?"

"To me it seems a splendid place, sir."

"The charm of inexperience is over your eyes. Now here" (he pointed to the leafy enclosure we had entered) "all is real, sweet, and pure."

DAWN 93

He wandered down a path edged with all kinds of flowers, as fresh now as a lovely spring morning could make them. The sun was just appearing, and its light fell on the dewy trees and the quiet walks beneath.

" Jane, will you have a flower? "

He gathered a half-open rose, the first on the bush, and offered it to me.

" You have passed a very strange night, Jane, and it has made you look pale. Were you afraid when I left you alone with Mason? "

" I was afraid of someone coming out of the inner room."

" But I had fastened the door: you were safe."

" Will Grace Poole live here still, sir? "

" Oh, yes! don't trouble yourself about her."

" Yet it seems to me that your life is hardly safe while she stays."

" Never mind . . . I will take care of myself."

" Is the danger that you feared last night gone now, sir? "

" I cannot be certain until Mason is out of England; nor even then."

" But Mr. Mason seems a man who is easily led. Your influence, sir, is obviously strong with him. He will never purposely harm you."

Mr. Rochester laughed bitterly, hastily took my hand, and as hastily threw it from him.

" Oh, no! He will not disobey me . . . but without intending it, he might in a moment, by one careless word, cause me to lose, if not my life, yet my only chance of happiness. I must keep him ignorant that harm to me is possible. Now you look puzzled; and I will puzzle you further. You are my little friend, are you not? "

" I like to serve you, sir, and to obey you in all that is right."

" Exactly: I see you do. I see genuine contentment in your face when you are helping me in what you call 'all that is right.' But if I told you to do what you thought was wrong, my friend would then turn to me, quiet and pale, and would say, 'No, sir, that is impossible.' Well, you too have power over me, and may harm me, and I dare not reveal my weak spot, lest, faithful and friendly though you are, you should strike me at once."

" If you have no more to fear from Mr. Mason than you have from me, sir, you are very safe."

"God grant it may be so! Here, Jane, is a seat. You don't hesitate to take a place by my side, do you? "

I felt that to refuse would be unwise.

"Well, Jane, I'll ask your advice. Suppose that you were no longer a well-brought-up girl, but a wild boy, spoilt from childhood. Imagine yourself in a distant foreign land; suppose that you there make a serious mistake, one whose results must follow you all through life. Remember, I don't say a *crime*: my word is *mistake*. Life becomes bitter and miserable: you wander here and there, seeking happiness in idle pleasure. Weary and dissatisfied, you come home after many years: you make a new acquaintance. You find in this stranger the good and bright qualities which you have sought for twenty years, in vain. You feel purer feelings coming back to you, and you wish to begin a new life. In order to do this, would you be right to disregard a custom which neither your conscience admits nor your judgment approves? Would it be right to dare the world's opinion in order to attach to you for ever this gentle stranger? "

He paused for an answer, and what was I to say? Oh, for some good spirit to suggest a wise and satisfactory reply.

"Sir," I answered. " No man's improvement should depend entirely upon a fellow-creature. He should look higher than his equals for strength to lead a better life."

" But the instrument! God, who does the work, chooses the instrument. I believe I have found the instrument for my own cure in . . ."

He paused: the birds went on singing, and the leaves lightly moving. At last I looked up at the speaker: he was looking eagerly at me.

" Little friend," said he, in quite a changed tone—while his face changed too, losing all its softness, and becoming hard

and mocking—" you have noticed my tender feeling for Miss
Ingram. Don't you think if I married her she would improve
me? "

He got up instantly, went quite to the other end of the path,
and when he came back he was humming a tune.

" She's a rare one, is she not, Jane? "

" Yes, sir."

" A real beauty, Jane. Why, there's Dent and Lynn in the
garden. Go back to the house by that side-gate."

As I went one way, he went another, and I heard him saying cheerfully :

" Mason was up before you this morning; he was gone before
sunrise : I rose at four to see him go."

CHAPTER 24

NEWS FROM GATESHEAD

ON the afternoon of this same day I was summoned downstairs
by a message that someone wanted me in Mrs. Fairfax's room.
There I found a man having the appearance of a gentleman's
servant, and dressed in black.

" I expect you hardly remember me, miss," he said, rising
as I entered, " but I was coachman with Mrs. Reed when you
were at Gateshead, and I live there still."

" Oh, how do you do? I remember you very well. And
how is Bessie? You are married to Bessie, are you not? "

" Yes, my wife is very well, thank you."

" And are the family well at the house? "

" I am sorry I can't give you better news of them, miss.
Mr. John died a week ago in London."

" Mr. John? "

" Yes. His life was very wild. He got into debt and into
prison : his mother helped him out twice, but the third time
she refused, and the next news was that he was dead. They
say he killed himself."

I was silent. The news was frightful. The coachman went on:

"Missis had been in poor health herself for some time. The loss of money and fear of poverty were troubling her. The shock of Mr. John's death was too sudden. She fell ill, and remained three days without speaking, but last Tuesday she seemed rather better, and kept making signs to Bessie and murmuring. At last my wife understood the words, 'Bring Jane Eyre: I want to speak to her.' She told Miss Reed and Miss Georgiana and advised them to send for you, and at last they agreed. If you can get ready, miss, I should like to take you back with me early to-morrow morning."

"Yes, I shall be ready: it seems to me that I ought to go."

Having directed him to the servants' hall, I went in search of Mr. Rochester. He was entertaining some of his guests. It required some courage to disturb the party, but my business was urgent. I approached my master where he stood at Miss Ingram's side. She turned as I drew near, and when I said, in a low voice, "Mr. Rochester," she made a movement, as if tempted to order me away.

Mr. Rochester followed me from the room.

"Well, Jane?" he said, as he rested his back against the schoolroom door, which he had shut.

"If you please, sir, I want permission to be absent for a week or two."

"What for? Where are you going?"

"To see a sick lady, my uncle's wife at Gateshead. She has sent for me."

"And what good can you do her? Nonsense, Jane! I would never think of running a hundred miles to see someone who will probably be dead before you reach her."

"I cannot be easy in my mind if I neglect her wishes."

"Promise me only to stay a week . . ."

"I had better not give my word: I might be obliged to break it."

"But you *will* come back? You will not be persuaded to remain permanently with her?"

" Oh, no!   I shall certainly return if all is well."

" Well, you must have some money; I have given you no salary yet.   How much have you in the world, Jane? "

I drew out my purse.

" Five shillings, sir."

He laughed, and searched his pockets.

" Here," he said, offering me a note for fifty pounds.   I told him I had no change.

" I don't want change; you know that.   Take your wages."

I refused to accept more than was due to me: he owed me only fifteen.

He looked angry at first; then, as if remembering something, he said:

" Right!   Right!   Better not give you all now: you would, perhaps, stay away three months. There are ten: that's plenty, isn't it? "

" Yes, sir, but you now owe me five."

" Come back for it."

" Mr. Rochester, I may as well mention another matter of business to you while I have the opportunity."

" Matter of business?   I am curious to hear it."

" You have informed me, sir, that you are shortly going to be married.   In that case, sir, Adele ought to go to school."

" To get her out of my bride's way?   And you? "

" I must seek another situation somewhere.   I must advertise."

" Of course! " he exclaimed, with a sharpness of tone and a twisting of his features unusual in him.   " You dare to advertise!   I wish I had only offered you a pound instead of ten.   Give me back nine pounds, Jane, I've a use for it."

" And so have I, sir," I returned, putting my hands and my purse behind me.

" Ungenerous little thing! " said he.   " Give me five pounds, Jane."

" Not five shillings, sir, nor five pence."

" Just let me look at the money."

" No, sir, you are not to be trusted."

" Jane! "

" Sir? "

" Promise me not to advertise, and to leave the finding of a situation to me."

" I shall be glad to do so, sir, if you, in your turn, will promise that Adele and I shall both be safely out of the house before your bride enters it."

" Very well!   You go to-morrow, then? "

" Yes, sir, early."

" Then you and I must say good-bye for a little while? "

" I suppose so, sir."

" And how do people perform that ceremony of parting? Teach me, Jane."

" They say, ' Good-bye,' or any other form they prefer."

" Then say it."

" Good-bye, Mr. Rochester, for the present."

" It seems dry, to me, and unfriendly. I should like something else. If one shook hands, for instance; but no—that would not content me either."

" How long is he going to stand with his back against that door? " I asked myself. " I want to begin packing."

The dinner-bell rang, and he rushed away without another word.

CHAPTER 25

MRS. REED'S SECRET

I REACHED Gateshead at about five o'clock in the afternoon, and went in first to see Bessie, who insisted on my having some tea. Old times crowded back into my mind as I watched her moving about, giving her children an occasional tap or push, just as she used to give me in former days. She still had her quick temper as well as her good looks.

After about an hour I walked with her towards the house which I had left, nearly nine years before, despairing and lonely. My future was doubtful still, and still I had an aching heart: I still felt a wanderer on the face of the earth, but I experienced firmer trust in myself and less dread of injustice. The wound of my wrongs, too, was now quite healed.

"You shall go into the breakfast-room first," said Bessie, "the young ladies will be there."

In another moment I was within that room. There was every article of furniture looking just as it did on the morning when I was first introduced to Mr. Brocklehurst: even the rug he had stood on still lay in front of the fire. Gazing at the bookcase, I thought I could see *Gulliver's Travels* in its old place on the third shelf.

The living creatures, however, had changed so much that I did not recognize them. Two young ladies appeared before me. One was very tall and thin, with a severe expression and extremely plain dress. This, I felt, must be Eliza. The other fair, with handsome and regular features, blue eyes and yellow hair, was Georgiana.

Both, as I advanced, rose to welcome me, and then, after the greeting, paid me no further attention, except that the younger one examined with a critical air the simple and unfashionable quality of my clothes.

Their neglect had no longer any power to hurt me, and when they seemed unwilling that I should see their mother immediately, I went without consulting them.

I did not need to be guided to the well-known room, to which I had so often been summoned for punishment in former days. I approached the bed and eagerly sought the familiar features. It is a happy thing that time ends the longing for vengeance and calms the feelings of rage and hatred. I bent down and kissed my aunt. She looked at me.

"Is this Jane Eyre?" she said.

"Yes, Aunt Reed. How are you, dear aunt?"

I had once sworn never to call her "aunt" again. I thought it no shame to forget this now. My fingers fastened on her hand which lay outside the sheet, but Mrs. Reed took the hand away, and turned her face from me.

I felt pain, and then I felt anger. My tears had risen, just as in childhood, but I checked them.

" You sent for me," I said, " and I am here."

" Oh, of course! Tell my daughters I wish you to stay until I can talk to you about something that is troubling me. There was something I wished to say . . . let me see . . ."

The wandering look and altered voice told what change had taken place in her once healthy form. Turning restlessly, she found my elbow resting on a corner of the sheet.

" Sit up! " she said, " don't annoy me with holding the sheet fast. Are you Jane Eyre? "

" I am Jane Eyre."

" I have had more trouble with that child than anyone would believe. Such a burden to be left on my hands! I was glad to get her away from the house. The fever broke out in Lowood. She did not die, but I said she did—I wish she had died! "

" Why do you hate her so, Mrs. Reed? "

" I had a dislike for her mother. My husband was so fond of his sister that he sent for her baby when she died. It was a weak thing, always crying. My husband used to take more notice of it than of his own children, and he was angry with them when they would not play with it. He made me promise to look after it. John is not like his father, and I am glad of it. Oh, I wish he would stop asking me for money! John spends dreadfully on cards, and always loses, poor boy! I have heavy troubles. What is to be done? "

By now she was getting much excited. Bessie with difficulty persuaded her to take some medicine. She grew calmer, and I left her.

More than ten days passed before I had any more conversation with her. I had little satisfaction in the society of my two cousins, but I had my drawing materials with me, and with them I occupied my time. Georgiana, after a time, was pleased to have me draw a picture of her, and to confide in me the various love affairs she had enjoyed in town two years before. Eliza spoke little, but occasionally quarrelled with her sister.

One wet, windy afternoon, Georgiana had fallen asleep over a novel, and Eliza had gone to church. I thought I would go upstairs and see how the dying woman was, who lay there half neglected, for the servants and nurse were lazy, her daughters did not care, and Bessie was occupied with her own family. I found the sick-room unattended, as I had expected.

The patient lay still, and I gazed on her who could now no longer gaze on me. I remembered Helen Burns, and was listening in imagination to her well-loved voice as she said her last words to me, when a weak murmur came from the bed:

"Who is that?"

I answered, but it was some time before Mrs. Reed could recognize me.

"I am very ill now," she said after a while. "It is better that I should relieve my mind before I die. What we think little of in health troubles us at such an hour as this is to me. Is there anyone else here?"

I assured her we were alone.

"Well, I have twice done you a wrong which I regret now. One was in breaking the promise which I gave my husband to bring you up as my own child; the other . . ." she stopped. "After all, it is of no great importance, perhaps," she murmured to herself, "and then I may get better, and to humble myself so to her is painful."

She made an attempt to move, but failed. Her face changed.

"Well, I must do it I had better tell her. Go to my writing-desk, open it, and take out a letter you will see there."

I obeyed her instructions.

"Read the letter," she said,

It was short, and as follows:

MADAM,

Will you have the goodness to send me the address of my niece, Jane Eyre, and to tell me how she is? It is my intention to write shortly and ask her to come and live with me in Madeira.[1] God has blessed me with prosperity, and as I am

---

[1] Madeira = the chief of a group of islands to the south-west of Portugal, famous for its wine.

unmarried and childless, I wish to adopt her and leave her at
my death whatever I may then possess.

I am, Madam,

Yours faithfully,

JOHN EYRE.

It was dated three years back.

" Why did I never hear of this? " I asked.

" Because I disliked you too deeply. I could not forget how
you once accused me of cruelty, and told me you hated me
the worst of anybody in the world. I took my revenge. I
wrote and told your uncle that Jane Eyre had died of fever at
Lowood. Now do as you please."

" Dear Mrs. Reed," I said, " think no more of all this. Forgive me for my passionate language : I was a child then. If
you could but be persuaded to think of me kindly . . ."

" You have a very bad nature," she replied, " and even now
I find it impossible to understand how for nine years you
could be patient under any treatment, and in the tenth break
out all fire and violence."

." I am not so bad as you think. Many a time, as a child,
I should have been glad to love you if you would have let me.
Kiss me, aunt."

I approached my cheek to her lips. She would not touch it.
Her hands were growing cold. Bessie entered. I waited half
an hour longer, but she made no sign. At twelve o'clock
that night she died.

CHAPTER 26

RETURN TO THORNFIELD

MR. ROCHESTER had given me only one week's holiday, but a
month passed before I left Gateshead. I wished to go immediately after the funeral, but was urged by my cousins to remain
until they had completed their arrangements for departure,
Georgiana to her uncle's home in London where she married

soon afterwards, Eliza to a religious house in France, where later she became a nun.

My journey seemed very long, and my mind was not at rest. I was returning to Thornfield, but how long was I going to stay there? I had heard from Mrs. Fairfax that the party at the Hall had ended, and Mr. Rochester had left for London, probably to make arrangements for his wedding, as he talked of buying a new carriage. He was expected back shortly.

I had not told Mrs. Fairfax the exact day of my return, for I did not wish the carriage to meet me at Millcote. I proposed to walk the distance quietly by myself, taking an old road through fields. It was a mild summer evening, and the haymakers were at work all along the way.

I walked on till I had only a field or two still to cross. The hedges were full of roses, but I had no time to gather any; I wanted to be at the house. I passed a tall bush; I saw the narrow stile with stone steps; and I saw Mr. Rochester sitting there, a book and pencil in his hand; he was writing.

For the moment I was unable to move. I did not think I should tremble in this way when I saw him, nor lose my voice in his presence. I wanted to go back and enter the house by another way; but I could not stir. Then it was useless; he had seen me.

"Hallo!" he cried, and he put down his book and pencil. "There you are! Come on, if you please!"

I came on, trying my best to appear calm.

"And is this Jane Eyre? Have you come from Millcote, and on foot? Yes . . . just one of your tricks, to come softly along to your home at twilight, as if you were a dream or a spirit. What have you been doing this last month?"

"I have been with my aunt, sir, who is dead."

"A true Janian reply! Good angels be my guard! She comes from the other world . . . from the land of the dead! If I dared, I'd touch you, to see if you are substance or shadow. Unfaithful!" he added, when he had paused for an instant. "Absent from me a whole month, and forgetting me quite, I'll be sworn!"

He did **not leave** the stile, and I hardly liked to ask to go by. I inquired soon if he had not been to London.

" Yes; I suppose Mrs. Fairfax told you the reason. You must see the carriage, Jane, and tell me if it won't suit Mrs. Rochester exactly. I wish, Jane, I were better matched with her in appearance. Tell me now, you fairy . . . can't you give me a charm to make me a handsome man? "

" It would be beyond the power of magic, sir," and, in thought, I added: " A loving eye is all the charm needed: to such you are handsome enough, or rather your sternness has a power beyond beauty."

Mr. Rochester had sometimes read my unspoken thoughts with a quickness that I could not understand. In the present instance he took no notice of my sharp words, but he smiled at me with a certain smile he had of his own, and which he used on but rare occasions. It was the real sunshine of feeling.

" Pass, Jane," he said, making room for me to cross the stile.

All I had to do now was to obey him in silence. I got over the stile without a word and meant to leave him calmly. But some force caused me to turn round, and I said, in spite of myself:

" Thank you, Mr. Rochester, for your great kindness. I am exceedingly glad to get back again to you."

I walked on so fast that even he could hardly have followed me if he had tried. Little Adele was half wild with delight when she saw me. Mrs. Fairfax received me with her usual plain friendliness, and even the servants smiled. This was very pleasant: it was the first time in my life that I had experienced the joy of coming home.

Two weeks of calm followed my return to Thornfield. Nothing was said of my master's marriage, and I saw no preparation going on for such an event. One thing especially surprised me, and that was that there were no journeyings backwards and forwards, no visits to Ingram Park. Nor could I ever remember the time when my master's face had been so cheerful. If, in the moments I and my pupil spent with him, I looked unhappy, he became even gay. Never had he called me more frequently to his presence, and alas! never had I loved him so well.

CHAPTER 27

THE STORM BREAKS

ON Midsummer evening, Adele, weary with gathering wild fruit, had gone to bed early. I watched her fall asleep, and when I left her I sought the garden.

It was now the sweetest hour of the twenty-four. Sunset was at meeting with moonrise. I found a winding path where I might wander unseen, but it was not long before my step was arrested—not by sound, not by sight, but by a warning scent. This new scent was neither of leaf nor flower; it was—I knew it well—Mr. Rochester smoking. I saw him in the distance, and I stepped aside to a sheltered seat. "If I sit still," I thought, "he will never see me."

He wandered about, now examining the fruit on the bushes, now bending towards a flowering plant. A great insect went humming by and settled near his foot: he saw it, and turned to examine it.

"Now he has his back towards me," I thought. "Perhaps if I walk softly, I can slip away unnoticed."

I trod gently on a grassy border, but as I crossed his shadow, cast long over the garden by the moon, he said quietly, without turning round:

"Turn back, Jane. On so lovely a night it is a shame to remain in the house."

It is one of my faults, that though my tongue is sometimes ready enough with an answer, there are times when it fails me sadly in making an excuse; and this weakness always occurs at some difficult moment, when some simple word is needed to get me out of painful embarrassment. It failed me now.

"Jane," he began again, as we entered an avenue, "Thornfield is a pleasant place in summer, is it not?   Would you not be sorry to part with it? "

" Must I leave, sir? " I asked.

" I am sorry, Jane, but I believe you must."

" Then you *are* going to be married, sir? "

" In about a month I hope to be a bridegroom. I have already, through my future mother-in-law, heard of a place that I think will suit you: it is to educate the five daughters of a lady in Western Ireland."

" It is a long way off, sir."

" Never mind—a girl of your sense will not object to the voyage or the distance. We have been good friends, Jane; have we not? "

" Yes, sir."

" It is unlikely that we shall meet again. I suppose that you will forget me? "

" That I *never* should, sir: you know . . ."   It was impossible to continue.

" Jane, do you hear that bird singing in the wood? "

In listening, I wept. I could hide my feelings no longer. When I did speak, it was to express a passionate wish that I had never been born, or never come to Thornfield.

The violence of emotion, stirred by grief and love within me, was claiming mastery, and demanding a right to overcome, and to speak.

" I love Thornfield—I love it, because I have lived in it a full and delightful life . . . for a little while at least. I have not been despised or ill-treated. I have talked, face to face, with what I delight in—with a strong and original mind. I have known you, Mr. Rochester, and I find it unbearable that I must be separated from you for ever. I see the necessity of departure, and it is like looking on the necessity of death."

" Where do you see the necessity? "

" You, sir, have placed it before me, in the form of your bride."

" My bride!   I have no bride! "

" But you will have."

" Yes. I will! I will! " He set his teeth.

" Then I tell you I must go! " I replied, roused to something like passion. " Do you think I can stay to become nothing to you? Do you think I am a machine without feelings? Do you think, because I am poor, humble, plain, and little, I am soulless and heartless? You think wrong! And if God had gifted me with some beauty and much wealth, I should have made it as hard for you to leave me, as it is now for me to leave you. I am not talking to you now by the standards of custom and the world; it is my spirit that addresses your spirit, as if we stood before God, equal, as we are! "

" As we are! " repeated Mr. Rochester. " So," he added, enclosing me in his arms. " So, Jane! "

" Yes, so, sir," I returned, " and yet not so, for you are about to marry a person who is inferior to you—one with whom you have no sympathy—whom I do not believe that you truly love. I would scorn such a union: therefore I am better than you— let me go! "

" Where, Jane? To Ireland? "

" Yes . . . to Ireland. I have said what I think, and can go anywhere now."

" Jane, be still; don't struggle so, like a wild bird."

" I am no bird. I am a free human being with an inde-pendent will, which I now use to leave you."

Another effort set me at liberty.

" And your will shall decide your fate," he said, " I offer you my hand, my heart, and a share of all my possessions."

I was silent: I thought he mocked me.

" Do you doubt me, Jane? "

" Entirely."

" You have no faith in me? "

" Not a bit."

" Am I a liar in your eyes? " he asked passionately. " Little unbeliever, you *shall* be convinced. What love have I for Miss Ingram? What love has she for me? None. I caused a story to reach her that my fortune was not a third of what was supposed, and when I visited her to see the result, it was coldness from her and her mother. I would not—I could not—marry Miss Ingram. I have only tried to make you jealous. You, I love you as myself. You—poor and humble, and small and plain as you are—I beg you to accept me as a husband."

I began—with his earnestness and especially his plain speaking—to believe in his sincerity.

"Do you truly love me? Do you really wish me to be your wife?"

"I do. I am willing to swear it."

"Then I will marry you."

He drew me to him. "Make my happiness—I will make yours. God pardon me! Let not man interfere with me: I have her, and will keep her."

"There is no one to interfere, sir. I have no relations."

"No—that is the best of it," he said. If I had loved him less, I might have thought his voice and look of triumph wild. "I know that my Creator approves what I do. For the world's judgment, I care nothing."

But what had happened to the night? The moon was clouded over, and wind roared in the avenue. A spark leapt out of the sky, and there was a crack, a crash.

"We must go in," said Mr. Rochester, "the weather is changing. I could have sat with you till morning, Jane."

The rain rushed down. He hurried me to the house. He was shaking the water from my dress when Mrs. Fairfax came out of her room. She looked pale, serious, and amazed. I only smiled at her and ran upstairs.

"Explanation will do for another time," I thought.

The storm continued all night, with thunder, lightning and rain. In the morning little Adele came running into my room to tell me that a great tree at the bottom of the garden had been struck by lightning and half of it split away.

CHAPTER 28

THE TORN VEIL

OUR wedding was to take place quietly in a month's time. Meanwhile, in spite of Mr. Rochester's opposition, I continued to work as Adele's governess, and refused to spend any time with him except the usual after-dinner hour. I resisted, too, his desire to buy me jewels and rich clothes, which reminded me too greatly of my poverty. In this connection I remembered what, in the hurry of events, I had forgotten—the letter of my uncle, John Eyre, to Mrs. Reed, and his intention of adopting me and making me his heir.[1]

" It would indeed be a relief," I thought, " if I had even a small independent income. I will write to my uncle and tell him I am alive and going to be married." And this I immediately did.

The month passed: its very last hours had come. All preparations for the bridal day were completed. My trunks were packed, locked, and waiting the fixing on of the address cards, on which Mr. Rochester had himself written the name, " Mrs. Rochester." Immediately after the ceremony we were to leave for Europe.

I felt restless and excited. It was not only the hurry of preparation that made me feverish, nor the thought of the new life that was to begin to-morrow. A third cause influenced my mind more than they.

My mind was troubled. Something had happened which I could not understand; no one knew of or had seen the event but myself. It had taken place the previous night, when Mr. Rochester was absent from home on business. I waited now for his return, eager to seek of him a solution to the problem.

At last he came. I found him at supper.

" Take a seat and share my meal, Jane. This is almost the last meal that you will eat at Thornfield Hall for a long time."

[1] heir, heiress = one who inherits.

I sat down near him, but told him I could not eat.

" Is it because you have the thought of a journey before you, Jane? What a bright spot of colour you have on each cheek! And how strangely your eyes glitter! Are you well? "

" I believe I am. I wish this present hour would never end. Who knows what fate may come with the next? "

" You are too excited, Jane, or you are tired out. Give me your confidence: relieve your mind of whatever is troubling it."

" Then, sir, listen. Last night, for some time after I went to bed, I could not sleep. A storm was rising, but beneath the noise it made I seemed to hear another sound, like the howling of some dog in the distance. When at last I slept, it was to dream that Thornfield Hall was a ruin."

" Is that all, Jane? "

" All the preface, sir; the tale is yet to come. On waking, a beam of light shone in my eyes. I thought it was daylight, but I was mistaken: it was only candle-light. The maid, I supposed, had come in. There was a light on the dressing-table, and the door of the cupboard, where, before going to bed, I had hung my wedding dress and veil, stood open. I heard a movement there. I asked, ' What are you doing? ' No one answered, but a form came out of the cupboard. It took the light, held it up, and examined the clothes there. I called out again, and still it was silent. I had risen up in bed, I bent forward. Surprise overcame me, and then my blood ran cold. Mr. Rochester, this was not a servant, it was not Mrs. Fairfax, it was not—no, I am sure of it—it was not even that strange woman, Grace Poole."

" It must have been one of them," interrupted my master.

" No, sir."

" Describe it, Jane."

" It seemed, sir, a woman, tall, with thick dark hair hanging down her back. Presently she picked up my veil and threw it over her own head. She gazed in the looking-glass, and I saw the reflection of her features in it. It was a fearful sight—unnatural, wild and coarse. Then, sir, she removed the veil, tore it in two, and throwing the pieces on the floor, trod upon them."

"And afterwards?"

"The figure retreated to the door. Just at my bedside it stopped, held the candle close to my face, and put it out under my eyes. I was aware of her face flaming over mine, and I lost consciousness: for the second time in my life I lost my senses from terror."

"Who was with you when you recovered?"

"No one. It was day. I rose and bathed my head and face in water. Though weak, I was not ill. I have kept this secret. Now, sir, tell me who and what that woman was."

"The invention of your excited brain, that is certain."

"I wish I could believe you, sir. But when on rising I looked round the room, there, on the carpet, I saw the veil, torn from top to bottom in two halves!"

I felt Mr. Rochester start.

"Thank God it was only the veil that was harmed! Now, Jane, I'll explain all about it. It was half dream, half reality. I have no doubt a woman did enter your room. It must have been Grace Poole. In a state between waking and sleeping, you got a false impression of her appearance. The tearing of the veil was real, and it is like her. You will ask why I keep such a woman in my house: when we have been married a year, I will tell you. Are you satisfied?"

I reflected. It appeared to be the only possible solution. I was not satisfied, but I tried to appear so, to please him.

"You must sleep in Adele's room to-night," said Mr. Rochester. "I would prefer that you did not sleep alone. Fasten the door on the inside. And now, Jane, no more gloomy thoughts."

I did not sleep much. A feeling of unreality would not be dismissed from my mind.

CHAPTER 29

THE MARRIAGE IS STOPPED

THE maid came at seven the next morning to dress me: she took a long time and when I went down Mr. Rochester was waiting impatiently at the foot of the stairs. He told me he would give me only ten minutes to eat some breakfast. Meanwhile he commanded the luggage and the carriage to be brought to the door.

" Jane, are you ready? "

I rose. There were no guests, no relations to wait for. Mr. Rochester hurried me out of the house at a rapid pace.

I can still remember the grey old church outside the gates, rising calm before me, with a red morning sky beyond. I have not forgotten, either, the figures of two strangers wandering about the churchyard, who passed round to the back when they saw us. By Mr. Rochester they were not observed: he was looking earnestly at my face.

We entered the quiet building, and took our places. The priest and the clerk were waiting, and the service began.

The explanation of the purpose and duties of marriage was read through, and then the clergyman came a step forward and, bending slightly towards Mr. Rochester, went on:

" I require and advise you both that if either of you know of any reason why you may not be lawfully united in marriage, you do now confess it."

He paused, as the custom is. When is the pause after that sentence ever broken by reply? Not, perhaps, once in a hundred years. The clergyman had not lifted his eyes from his book; he had waited only a moment, and was continuing, when a voice near by said:

" The marriage cannot go on: I declare the existence of a hindrance."

The priest looked at the speaker; it was one of the strangers whom I had noticed earlier. Mr. Rochester moved slightly and, standing more firmly, said:

"Go on."

The priest answered: "I cannot go on without first inquiring into what has been said, and receiving proof of its truth or otherwise."

"The ceremony must be broken off," repeated the voice behind us. "I am in a position to prove my statement."

The priest hesitated.

"What is the nature of the hindrance? Perhaps it may be explained away?"

"Hardly," was the answer. Pronouncing each word distinctly, calmly, steadily, the speaker continued:

"It simply consists in the existence of a previous marriage. Mr. Rochester has a wife still living."

I looked at Mr. Rochester: I made him look at me. His whole face was like colourless rock: his eye both spark and steel. Without speaking, without smiling, he only encircled my waist with his arm and held me to his side.

"Who are you?" he asked the stranger.

"My name is Briggs. I am a lawyer."

"And you claim that I have a wife?"

"I remind you of the lady's existence, sir, which the law recognizes, if you do not."

"Give me an account of her—her name, her family."

"Certainly."

Mr. Briggs took a paper from his pocket and read in a calm voice:

"'I state and can prove that Edward Rochester, of Thornfield Hall, was married to my sister, Bertha Mason, at Spanish Town, Jamaica, fifteen years ago. The details of the marriage will be found in the church records there. A copy is now in my possession. Signed, Richard Mason.'"

"If that is a genuine statement, it may prove that I have been married, but it does not prove that the woman mentioned in it is still living."

"She was living three months ago. I have a witness to the fact."

"Where is he?"

"He is on the spot. Mr. Mason, have the goodness to step forward."

Mr. Rochester, on hearing the name, set his teeth. I felt a quiver of fury or despair run through him. The second stranger, who had till now remained in the shadows, approached. A pale face looked over the lawyer's shoulder—it was Mason himself. Mr. Rochester turned and fixed him with his gaze. He stirred, lifted his strong arm—he could have struck Mason, dashed him to the church floor, but the man drew back trembling, and cried out faintly.

"Sir," said the priest, "do not forget you are in a holy place." Then, addressing Mason, he inquired gently, "Are you aware, sir, if this gentleman's wife is still living?"

"She is now living at Thornfield Hall," said Mason, in a low, hesitating voice. "I saw her there last April."

"At Thornfield Hall!" exclaimed the priest. "Impossible! I have lived many years in this neighbourhood, sir, and never heard of a Mrs. Rochester there."

I saw a bitter smile twist Mr. Rochester's lips, and he said between his teeth:

"No, by God! I took care that none should hear of her under that name." He was silent for some minutes, and then went on, "Enough! All shall be revealed at once. Close your book. There will be no wedding to-day."

And Mr. Rochester began his story.

CHAPTER 30

MR. ROCHESTER'S STORY

"I AM little better than a devil at this moment, and deserve no doubt the sternest judgments of God. Gentlemen, my plan is broken up. What this lawyer and his witness say is true.

The clergyman here says he has never heard of a Mrs. Rochester at the Hall, but I suppose he has listened at some time or other to talk about the mysterious madwoman kept there under lock and key. I now inform you that she is my wife, sister of this brave-hearted person here, with his white cheeks and trembling limbs. Bertha Mason is mad, and she came of a mad family, weak-minded and violent. Her mother was both a madwoman and a heavy drinker—as I found out after I had married the daughter, for they were silent on family secrets before. Bertha copied her parent in both points.

"My father was to blame for this. I was not the eldest son. I once had a brother older than I. My father was not a generous man, and could not bear the idea of dividing his property so as to leave me a fair share. All, he resolved, should go to my brother. Yet he could not bear that a son of his should be a poor man. I must be provided for by a wealthy marriage. Mr. Mason, a West India merchant, was an old acquaintance of his. He had a son and daughter, and my father learnt that he would give the daughter a fortune of thirty thousand pounds. That was enough for my father. When I left college, I was sent out to Jamaica, to marry a bride already chosen for me. My father said nothing about her money, but he told me that Miss Mason was the pride of Spanish Town for her beauty, and this was no lie. I found her a fine woman, in the style of Blanche Ingram. They showed her to me at parties, splendidly dressed. I seldom saw her alone, and had very little private conversation with her. All the men seemed to admire her and envy me. I was attracted, and being ignorant, young and inexperienced, I thought I loved her. Her relations encouraged me; rivals made me jealous; and a marriage was accomplished almost before I knew it.

"Later, the truth was made known to me. My wife's beauty turned to coarseness, and her weaknesses developed to their worst extent. Meanwhile my brother died, and at the end of four years my father died also. I was rich now, and yet in happiness poorer than a slave.

"I brought my so-called wife to England, and had a fearful

voyage with such a creature on the vessel. I hired Grace Poole to keep watch over her. She and the surgeon Carter are the only two I have ever admitted to my confidence. Mrs. Fairfax may have suspected something, but she could have had no exact knowledge of the facts. Grace has, on the whole, proved a good keeper, though owing to an occasional tendency to drinking, she has once or twice allowed her patient to escape.

" But I owe you no further explanation. Gentlemen, I invite you to come up to the house and visit Mrs. Poole's patient, and my wife! This girl," he continued, looking at me, " knew nothing of the disgusting secret. She thought all was fair and lawful. Come, all of you—follow! "

Still holding me fast, he left the church. The three gentlemen came after. At the front door of the Hall we found the carriage.

" Take it back to the coach-house," said Mr. Rochester, " it will not be wanted to-day."

At our entrance, Mrs. Fairfax, Adele, and the servants advanced to greet us.

" Away with your congratulations! " cried the master. " Who wants them? Not I! They are fifteen years too late."

He passed on and ascended the stairs to the third storey. The low, black door, opened by his key, admitted us to the room where Mason had lain wounded. He opened the inner door and we entered.

In a room without a window there burnt a fire guarded by high, strong bars. A lamp hung from the roof by a chain. Grace Poole bent over the fire cooking something in a pot. In the deep shade at the farthest end of the room, a figure ran backwards and forwards. What it was, whether beast or human being, one could not, at first sight, tell. It crawled, seemingly, on the floor; it made strange animal-like noises, but it was covered with clothing, and a quantity of dark, grey hair hid its face and head.

" Good morning, Mrs. Poole," said Mr. Rochester. " How is your patient to-day? "

"Moderate, sir," replied Grace, lifting the boiling pot carefully off the fire.

A fierce cry seemed to deny the truth of her report. The clothed animal rose, and stood upright.

"Ah, sir, she sees you!" exclaimed Grace, "you'd better not stay. For God's sake, take care!"

The madwoman roared: she pushed her disordered hair back from her face, and gazed wildly at her visitors. I recognized those coarse features. Mrs. Poole advanced.

"Keep out of the way," said Mr. Rochester. "she has no knife now, I suppose, and I'm watching."

"Take care!" cried Grace.

The three gentlemen retreated together. Mr. Rochester pushed me behind him. The madwoman sprang and seized his throat fiercely, and laid her teeth to his cheek. They struggled. She was a big woman, in height almost equalling her husband, and strong besides. He could have settled her with a well-directed blow, but he would not strike. At last he mastered her arms, and tied her to a chair with some rope. The operation was performed amid the fiercest screams. Mr. Rochester then turned to the spectators, with a smile both bitter and despairing.

"That is my wife," he said, "and this is what I wished to have" (laying his hand on my shoulder), "this young girl who stands so calm and quiet. Look at the difference, then judge me if you can."

We all left the room except Mr. Rochester, who stayed behind for a moment to give some further order to Grace Poole. The lawyer addressed me as he descended the stair.

"You, madam," he said, "are cleared from all blame. Your uncle will be glad to hear it—if, indeed, he still should be living."

"My uncle! Do you know him?"

"Mr. Mason does. Mr. Eyre has been the Madeira agent of his business for some years. When your uncle received your letter mentioning the coming marriage between yourself and Mr. Rochester, Mr. Mason happened to be staying with

At last he mastered her arms. (Page 117)

him. Mr. Eyre told him the news, for he knew that Mr. Mason was acquainted with a Mr. Rochester. Mr. Mason, astonished and troubled, revealed the real state of affairs. Your uncle, who, I am sorry to say, is now very ill, and unlikely to recover, could not hurry to England himself to save you from the trap into which you had fallen, but he begged Mr. Mason to return here at once to try to prevent the false marriage. Were I not certain that your uncle will be dead before you could reach Madeira, I would advise you to accompany Mr. Mason back there. As it is, I think you had better remain in England till you hear further, either from Mr. Eyre himself or from me. Have we anything else to stay for? " he inquired of Mr. Mason.

"No, no—let us be gone," was the anxious reply, and without waiting to speak to Mr. Rochester, they went out of the front door.

I stood at the half-open door of my own room, to which I had now retreated. The house was cleared; I shut myself in, fastened the bolt, and began not to weep, for I was still too calm for that—to take off the wedding dress, and replace it by the simple garment I had worn the day before, as I thought, for the last time. I then sat down: I felt weak and tired. I leaned my arms on a table, and my head dropped on them. Till now, I had only heard, seen, moved, watched event follow event: now, I thought.

Jane Eyre, who had been an eager, happy woman—almost a bride—was a cold, lonely girl again: her hopes were all dead. That bitter hour cannot be described: in truth, I came into deep waters, and the floods covered me.

CHAPTER 31

FLIGHT

SOME time in the afternoon I raised my head, and looking round, asked myself: " What am I to do? "

But the answer my mind gave: " Leave Thornfield at once."

was so immediate, so dreadful, that I closed my ears to it. I could not do it. But then a voice within me repeated that I could and must. I struggled with my own resolution. Conscience and passion fought until, weak with emotion and hunger, I fell asleep.

It was soon after midnight that I rose, and taking nothing but my purse and a small bundle, went softly from my room. I would have gone past Mr. Rochester's room without a pause, but my heart for a moment stopped its beat at the door, and my foot was forced to stop also. I heard him walking about restlessly within. He would send for me in the morning: I should be gone. He would suffer, perhaps grow despairing. I hesitated, and then moved on.

From the kitchen I got some water and some bread. Without a sound I opened the door and passed outside.

A mile off, beyond the fields, lay a road which stretched in the opposite direction to Millcote, a road I had never travelled along but often noticed. Towards this I directed my steps.

I walked on and on. The short summer night was nearly over, and birds began to sing in the hedges. Birds were faithful to their mates. And I? I was hateful to myself. Still, I could not turn back. God must have led me on. I was weeping wildly as I walked along, fast, fast, like one out of her mind. A weakness at length seized me, and I fell.

I lay on the ground for some minutes. I had some fear—or hope—that I should die, but I was soon up again, determined as ever to reach the road.

When I got there, I heard wheels, and saw a coach coming along. I stopped it, and asked to be taken as far as the pound in my purse would pay for. The interior was empty. I entered, and the coach rolled on its way.

CHAPTER 32

DESPAIR

It was evening when the coach set me down at a place where four roads met. It drove on: it was a mile away by now . . . I was alone. At this moment I discovered that I had forgotten to take my bundle out of the coach. I had nothing left in the world.

The signpost told me that the nearest town was ten miles off. There were great hills behind and on each side of me; there were ranges of mountains far beyond the deep valley at my feet. I saw no travellers on the road.

What was I to do? Where should I go? I touched the grass: It was dry, and still warm with the heat of the sun. The sky was clear, and there was no wind. To-night I would be the guest of Nature: she would lodge me without charge. I had one piece of bread left. I gathered a handful of wild fruit and ate it with the bread. I had some rest that night, but it was broken by a sad heart.

The next day, I followed a road which led away from the hot sun. Weariness had almost overcome me when I heard a bell—a church bell. Human life and human activity were near. A little later I entered a village. At the bottom of its one street there was a little shop with some bread in the window.

I went into the shop: a woman was there. Seeing a respectably dressed person, a lady as she supposed, she came forward with politeness. How could she serve me? I was seized with shame—for I had no money. My tongue would not pronounce the request for food which I had prepared. I only begged permission to sit down for a minute. Disappointed, she coldly pointed to a chair. I sank into it.

After a little while, I asked if there was any dressmaker in the village.

"Yes, two or three. Quite as many as there is employment for."

"Do you know of any place in the neighbourhood where a servant is wanted?"

"No, I do not."

I went on a little longer, but she seemed tired of my questions.

At last I took out my handkerchief, and asked if she would give me a loaf of bread for it.

She looked at me with immediate suspicion.

"No, I never sell stuff in that way. How can I tell where you got it?"

An ordinary beggar is often an object of distrust, a well-dressed one is always so. I could not blame the woman. I fled from the village in despair. The rest of the day I begged, but always in vain.

I passed the night in a wood. It was damp, and towards morning it rained. Another day went by, as hopeless as the first. I began to long for death.

Towards the evening on the next day, I saw a dim light in the distance, and dragged my weary limbs slowly in its direction. A white gate was just visible in the growing darkness. I passed through it and came to a kitchen window. A candle was burning on a table, and an elderly woman, somewhat rough-looking, but very clean, was sewing by its light.

A group of greater interest appeared near the fireside. Two young, graceful women—ladies in every way—sat, one in an armchair, the other on a lower seat. Both were dressed in black. A large old dog rested its head on the knee of one girl—the other girl was stroking a black cat.

This humble kitchen was a strange place for such people! Who were they? I had nowhere seen such faces as theirs, and yet, as I gazed at them, I seemed familiar with every feature. They were pale and thoughtful-looking, and each bent over a book, while two other great books, which they frequently consulted, lay on the floor beside them; those might be dictionaries to aid them in the task of translation.

I watched them for a long time. At last the elderly woman began to prepare a meal. I went to the door and knocked. She opened it.

"What do you want?" she inquired, in a voice of surprise.

"May I speak to your mistresses?"

"You had better tell me what you have to say to them. Where do you come from?"

"I am a stranger."

"What is your business here at this hour?"

"I want a night's shelter in a shed or anywhere, and a bit of bread to eat."

Distrust, the very feeling I dreaded, appeared in the woman's face. "I'll give you a piece of bread," she said, after a pause, "but we can't take a vagabond in to lodge."

"Where shall I go if you drive me away?"

"I expect you know where to go. Here is a penny. Move off."

Here the honest but unsympathetic servant shut the door and bolted it inside.

This was the end.

Weak as I was, I could not go another step. I sank down outside the door and wept.

"I can but die," I said aloud. "Let me wait God's will in silence."

"All men must die," said a voice quite near by, "but all are not condemned to do so in their youth."

"Who is speaking?" I asked, terrified at the unexpected sound. The newcomer knocked loudly at the door.

"Is it you, Mr. St. John?" cried the servant.

"Yes—yes; open quickly, Hannah."

"Well, how wet and cold you must be on a night like this! Come in—your sisters have been quite anxious about you. There has been a beggar-woman—I believe she has not gone yet! Get up, for shame!"

"Be silent, Hannah. You have done your duty, now let me do mine. I think this is a special case." And turning to me, he told me to pass before him into the house.

I obeyed him with difficulty. Presently I was within that clean, bright kitchen, with all the family gazing at me. My head swam: I dropped, but a chair received me. One of the sisters broke some bread, dipped it in milk, and put it to my lips. There was pity in her face. I tasted what was offered me: weakly at first, then more eagerly.

"No more at present, Diana. She has no strength: it will harm her. Try if she can speak now. Ask her her name."

I answered: "My name is Jane Elliott." I was anxious to avoid discovery.

"Where do you live? Where are your friends?"

I was silent.

"Can you send for anyone you know?"

I shook my head.

Somehow, now that I had once entered this house and been brought face to face with its owners, I no longer felt a wanderer who belonged nowhere. I ceased to feel a beggar, and my natural manner began to come back to me. When Mr. St. John demanded an account of myself, I said after a short pause:

"Sir, I can give you no details to-night."

"What, then, do you expect me to do for you?"

"Nothing." I had only enough strength for short answers.

Diana now spoke. "Do you mean that you have now received the aid that you require, and that we may dismiss you to the rainy night?"

I looked at her. She had, I thought, a remarkable face, expressive of both power and goodness. I took sudden courage. Answering her sympathetic gaze with a smile, I said:

"I will trust you. If I were a masterless and homeless dog, I know you would not turn me away to-night. As it is, I have no fear. Do as you like with me, but excuse me from much speech—it hurts me to use my voice."

All three looked at me in silence.

"Hannah," said Mr. St. John at last, "let her sit there at present, and ask her no questions. In ten minutes more, give her the rest of the bread and milk. Mary and Diana, let us go into the sitting-room and discuss the matter."

They went out. Very soon one of the ladies returned and gave some instructions to Hannah. Before long I was helped upstairs into a warm, dry bed. I thanked God, and in a glow of grateful joy fell fast asleep.

CHAPTER 33

THE RIVERS FAMILY

THE memory of three days and nights following this is very dim in my mind. I knew I was in a small room and in a narrow bed. I observed when anyone entered or left: I could understand what was said when they were near me; but to open my lips or move my limbs was impossible.

Hannah, the servant, was my most frequent visitor. I felt that she was prejudiced against me. Diana and Mary appeared once or twice a day. They would whisper sentences at my bedside, expressing curiosity as to who I might be, and thankfulness that they had not failed to give me shelter. Never once in their conversation did I hear a word of regret at the kindness they had shown me, or of suspicion or dislike of myself. I was comforted.

Mr. St. John came only once. He looked at me, and said my state of weakness was the result of excessive and continued weariness. He said that it was unnecessary to send for a doctor: " Nature will manage best left to herself. There is no disease." These opinions he stated in a few words, in a quiet, low voice. He stood observing me for some minutes, then added:

" She looks sensible, but not at all handsome."

On the third day I was better; on the fourth I could speak, move, sit up in bed, and turn. I began to have an appetite, and when in the afternoon I found on a chair by me all my own clothes, cleaned of the mud of my wanderings, I succeeded with some difficulty in dressing myself. Feeling once more respectable, I crept down some stone stairs and found my way to the kitchen.

Hannah was baking. When she saw me come in tidy and well dressed, she looked more approving. She even smiled.

" Well, you have got up! " she said. " You are better, then. You may sit in my chair by the fire, if you will."

She moved about busily, examining me occasionally out of the corner of her eye. Turning to me as she took some bread from the stove, she asked :

" Did you ever go begging before you came here? "

I was annoyed for a moment, but remembering how I had first appeared to her, I answered quietly and firmly :

" You are mistaken in supposing me a beggar. I am no more so than yourself or your young ladies."

After a pause she said :

" I don't understand : you have no house or money, I imagine? "

" The lack of house or money does not make me a beggar in your meaning of the word."

" Are you educated? " she inquired presently.

" Yes."

She opened her eyes wide.

" Then why cannot you support yourself? "

" I have supported myself, and I hope shall do so again. And now, never mind what I have been, but tell me the name of the family whom you serve."

" Their name is Rivers."

" Does the gentleman live here? "

" No, he is only staying a little while. He is a clergyman, and works at Morton, a few miles away."

" Their father is dead? "

" Yes, he died three weeks ago."

" They have no mother? "

" She has been dead many years. I have been here for thirty years, and looked after all three."

"That proves that you have been an honest and faithful servant. I say that in your favour, though you had the rudeness to call me a beggar, and refused me help when I was in trouble."

She gave me a look of surprise.

"I believe I was mistaken," she said, "you must not think too badly of me."

I continued rather severely:

"But I *do* think badly of you—not so much because you refused me shelter, but because you accused me of having no possessions. You should not consider poverty a crime."

"That is true," she admitted, "Mr. St. John told me so, too. I see I was wrong."

"Enough. I forgive you now. Shake hands."

She put out her rough hand and smiled. From that moment we were friends.

Hannah was a great talker, and as she worked she told me the history of the Rivers family. Their father had been a gentleman of good family, who had lost a great deal of money by trusting a man who gave him bad advice. As he was not rich enough to give his daughters fortunes, they had taken places as governesses. They were only now at home for a few weeks on account of their father's death. To be united and in their own house was their greatest happiness.

Presently the two ladies, who had been out for a walk to Morton, returned, accompanied by their brother. Mr. St. John, when he saw me, merely bowed and passed through the kitchen, but his sisters stopped. Mary quietly expressed the pleasure she felt in seeing me able to come down: Diana took my hand and shook her head at me.

"You should have waited for my permission to descend," she said, "you still look very pale. And why are you in here? Mary and I sit in the kitchen sometimes, because at home we like to be free, but you are a visitor, and must go into the sitting-room."

Still holding my hand, she made me rise, and led me into the inner room. She closed the door, leaving me alone with

Mr. St. John, who sat opposite me reading. I examined both him and the room.

The sitting-room was rather small and plainly furnished. Everything looked both well worn and well cared for. Mr. St. John, still as a statue, was young, perhaps from twenty-eight to thirty, with pure, straight features. His eyes were blue, his forehead high and colourless, his hair fair. He gave an impression, not of gentleness, but of hidden force. He did not speak one word to me till his sisters returned, bringing tea.

I ate eagerly. Mr. Rivers now closed his book and directed his eyes full upon me.

" You are very hungry," he said.

" I trust I shall not eat long at your expense, sir," was my awkward reply.

" No," he said coolly, " when you have told us the address of your friends, we can write to them, and you can go back to them."

" That, I must tell you plainly, is impossible."

The three looked at me, not with distrust, but with curiosity. I speak particularly of the ladies. St. John's eyes seemed to be less able to express his own thoughts than to search out those of others.

" Do you mean to say that you are completely without family? "

" I do."

" You are not married? " He looked quickly at my hands before he spoke.

As I replied to this, I felt a burning glow mount to my face. They all saw my embarrassment and emotion. Diana and Mary relieved me by turning their eyes elsewhere, but their colder and sterner brother continued to gaze.

" Where did you live last? " he now asked.

" You are too curious, St. John," murmured Mary in a low voice.

" That is my secret," I replied shortly.

" Which, in my opinion, you have a right to keep from everybody, if you wish," remarked Diana.

" If I know nothing of you and your history, I cannot help you," he said. " And you need help, do you not? "

" I need assistance from some good person in finding work that I can do, and that will enable me to keep myself."

" Tell me, then, what you *can* do."

" Mr. Rivers," I said, turning to him, and looking at him openly, " you and your sisters have done me a great service. You have a certain claim, not only on my gratitude, but also on my confidence. I will tell you as much about myself as I can without harming my own peace of mind, and the private affairs of myself and others.

" I am an orphan, educated at Lowood Institution. I left it nearly a year ago to become a governess. I was obliged to leave my situation last week for a reason that I cannot explain. No blame attached to me. I thought only of speed and secrecy in my departure, and in my troubled state of mind I neglected to take out of the coach by which I travelled the small amount of my possessions that I was able to bring away with me. In this position I found myself helpless and with failing strength, until you, Mr. Rivers, took me under the shelter of your roof."

" Don't make her talk any more, St. John," said Diana, as I paused, " she is clearly not yet fit for excitement. Come to the fire and sit down now, Miss Elliott."

I gave a start. I had forgotten my new name. Mr. Rivers, whom nothing seemed to escape, noticed it at once.

" You said your name was Jane Elliott? " he observed.

" I did say so, and it is the name by which I think it wise to be called at present."

" You would not like to be our guest for very long? "

" All I ask is that you will show me some means of getting work. Till then, allow me to stay here. I dread to be homeless again."

" Indeed you *shall* stay here," said Diana. " You *shall*," repeated Mary.

" My sisters, you see, have a pleasure in keeping you," said Mr. St. John. " *I* prefer to put you in a position to support yourself, and shall try to do so, but I work in a poor district, and my aid must be of the humblest sort."

I repeated my willingness to accept any means of employment that he might offer me, and soon after returned upstairs, for I had nearly come to the end of my strength again.

CHAPTER 34

DIANA, MARY, AND ST. JOHN

THE more I knew of Diana and Mary the better I liked them. In a few days I had recovered my health sufficiently to sit up all day, and walk out sometimes. I could join the sisters in all their occupations, and in doing this I now enjoyed for the first time the pleasure arising from perfect agreement in tastes, feelings and ideas.

They loved their home and the wild country around it, and I too soon learned to feel the attraction of the place. Indoors we agreed equally well. I liked to read what they liked to read. They were both more accomplished than I, but I followed with eagerness the path of knowledge that they had trodden before me. Diana offered to teach me German, and I in turn gave lessons in drawing to Mary. Thus occupied, days passed like hours, and weeks like days.

As to Mr. St. John, the close friendship which had arisen between me and his sisters did not include him. One reason was that he was seldom at home: he spent a great deal of his time in visiting the sick and poor in his neighbourhood. No bad weather seemed to keep him from these priestly duties.

But besides his frequent absences, there was another hindrance to friendship with him. He seemed of a lonely nature, living a life apart. The first real sign of his character came when I heard him preach in his own church. He spoke with calmness that grew into force. My heart was stirred, my mind astonished, by his words, but neither was softened.

Meanwhile a month had gone by. Diana and Mary were

soon to return to their posts in the south of England. St. John had said nothing to me about my future, and this problem was now becoming urgent.

One morning, being left alone with him for a few minutes, I ventured to approach the corner of the sitting-room which was kept specially for his use. I hesitated to begin, but he saved me the trouble.

Looking up as I drew near, he said:

" You have a question to ask me? "

" Yes, I wish to know whether you have heard of any employment for me."

" I found something for you three weeks ago, but as you seemed both happy and useful here, and your society gave my sisters unusual pleasure, I judged it unnecessary to break in on your comfort till their departure should make yours necessary."

" What is the work you have found for me? "

" It is nothing very profitable, but I consider that no service which can better our race is degrading. I believe you will accept it for a time, though I do not think it will satisfy your nature permanently."

" Do explain," I urged.

" I will. I shall not stay long at Morton now that my father is dead, but while I am there I shall do my best to improve it. I have already established a school for poor boys, and I mean now to open a second one for girls. I have hired a building, with a cottage for the school-mistress. Her salary will be thirty pounds a year. A rich lady in the neighbourhood is helping with expenses. Will you be the school-mistress? "

" I thank you for the proposal, Mr. Rivers, and I accept it with all my heart."

" But you understand me? It is a village school; your pupils will be only poor girls—labourers' and farmers' daughters. Sewing, reading, writing, simple arithmetic, will be all you will have to teach. What will you do with your accomplishments? "

" Save them till they are wanted. They will keep."

He smiled now, well pleased.

Diana and Mary became sadder and more silent as the day approached for leaving their brother and their home. As if to prove the old saying that " misfortunes never come singly," news came at this time to add to their disappointments. St. John entered one day with a letter.

" Your Uncle John is dead," he said. " Read."

Both sisters did so in silence. All smiled rather sadly.

" After all, we are no poorer than we were before," remarked Mary.

Diana turned to me.

" Jane, you will be surprised at us and our mysteries," she said, " and think us hard-hearted creatures for not feeling more at the death of so near a relation, but we have never seen or known him. He was our mother's brother. My father and he quarrelled because it was through his advice that my father lost all his money. They parted in anger and were never friends afterwards. He prospered, but did not marry. My father always hoped that he would put right the wrong that he had done, by leaving us his possessions. This letter informs us that he has left everything to his only other relation. He had a right, of course, to do as he pleased, yet we cannot help feeling for the moment a little disappointed. Even a small sum of money would have made a great deal of difference to us."

This explanation given, the subject was not mentioned any more. The next day I left to begin my new life, and the sisters departed for the south.

CHAPTER 35

THE VILLAGE SCHOOL

I CARRIED on the work of the village school as actively and faithfully as I could. It was truly hard at first. Some time passed before I could understand my pupils and their nature.

Entirely untaught, they seemed at first sight hopelessly dull, but I soon found I was mistaken. Many of them had excellent intelligence, and began to take a pleasure in doing their work well. The rapidity of their progress was sometimes surprising, and I felt an honest and happy pride in it. Their parents showed me respect and gratitude, and in time I felt I was becoming popular in the neighbourhood.

Yet, after a day spent in honourable labour among my pupils, and an evening spent in drawing or reading contentedly alone, I used to rush into strange dreams at night—stormy dreams, where, amidst unusual scenes, full of adventure, I again and again met Mr. Rochester, always at some exciting moment, and the hope of passing my life by his side would return, with all its first force and fire. Then I awoke, and the still, dark night witnessed my despair.

One day, it was a holiday: my house was tidy, and I sat in the afternoon drawing, when, after one rapid tap, my door opened, admitting St. John Rivers.

" I have come to see how you are spending your free time," he said. " Not, I hope, in thought? No, that is well: while you draw you will not feel lonely. I have brought you a book for the evening."

While I was eagerly looking through the pages, St. John bent to examine my drawing. When he had finished he drew over it the sheet of thin paper on which I was accustomed to rest my hand in painting, to prevent the cardboard from being stained. What he saw on this blank paper, it was impossible for me to tell; but something attracted his attention. He picked it up, and gave me a look, inexpressibly peculiar, and quite beyond my understanding. His lips opened as if to speak: but he checked the coming sentence, whatever it was.

" What is the matter? "

" Nothing in the world," was the reply, and, replacing the paper, I saw him neatly tear a narrow strip from the edge. It disappeared into his pocket, and, with one hasty nod and " good afternoon," he vanished.

I, in my turn, examined the paper, but saw nothing on it

except a few dull stains of paint. I puzzled over the mystery for a minute or two, but finding no explanation, I soon dismissed it from my mind.

CHAPTER 36

HEIRESS

WHEN St. John went, it was beginning to snow. The storm continued all night. A keen wind the next day brought fresh falls, and by twilight it was almost impossible to move out of doors. My astonishment, therefore, was very great when the door suddenly opened and St. John Rivers appeared, his tall figure almost covered with snow.

" Is there any bad news? " I asked. " Has anything happened? "

" No. How very easily you are alarmed! " he answered, removing his coat and shaking the snow from his boots. " I am spoiling your clean floor, but you must excuse me for once."

" But why have you come? "

" Rather an embarrassing question to put to a visitor. I merely wished to have a talk with you. Since yesterday I have been experiencing the excitement of a person to whom a tale has been half told, and who is impatient to hear its ending."

He sat down, and I waited, but he seemed occupied with his thoughts. I went on with the reading which his entrance had interrupted. Presently he took a letter from his pocket, looked at it in silence, and finally spoke.

" Leave your book a moment, and come a little nearer the fire."

Wondering, I obeyed.

" A little while ago," he went on, " I spoke of a half-finished story. I am going to repeat it to you. It is but fair to warn you that some of it will sound familiar.

" Twenty years ago, a poor priest—never mind his name—loved a rich man's daughter. She returned his love, and married him against the advice of all her friends. Before two years had passed, both were dead. They left a daughter, a friendless thing, unwillingly brought up by an aunt-in-law, called Mrs. Reed of Gateshead. You start—did you hear a noise? The orphan passed at the age of ten to a place you know—Lowood School, where she left an honourable record as a pupil and a teacher. She became a governess at the house of a certain Mr. Rochester."

"Mr. Rivers!" I interrupted.

"I have nearly finished. I know nothing of Mr. Rochester, except that he pretended to offer honourable marriage to this young girl, and that at the last moment she found out that he had a wife still alive, though a madwoman. Soon after, an event occurred which made inquiry after the governess necessary. It was then discovered that she had gone—no one could tell when, where, or how. All search after her was in vain. Yet it has become a matter of serious urgency that she should be found: advertisements have been put in all the papers. I myself have received a letter from a certain Mr. Briggs, a lawyer, giving me these details."

"But tell me," I said, "what about Mr. Rochester? Is he well?"

"I am ignorant of all concerning Mr. Rochester, except for his attempt to deceive the law."

"But these people wrote to him?"

"Mr. Briggs states that the answer to his application for information was signed by a lady: Alice Fairfax. This Rochester must have been a bad man," observed Mr. Rivers.

"You don't know him—don't pronounce an opinion on him," I said.

St. John took from his pocket a strip of paper marked with paint stains. I read on it, in my own handwriting, the words "Jane Eyre," doubtless written in some careless moment.

"Briggs wrote to me of a Jane Eyre," he said, "and the advertisements demanded someone of that name. I knew a Jane Elliott, and I had my suspicions. This piece of paper convinced me yesterday. You admit to your real name?"

"Yes, but where is Mr. Briggs? Perhaps he knows more of Mr. Rochester than you do."

"Mr. Briggs is in London, but I doubt whether he is interested in Mr. Rochester. You do not inquire why he is interested in *you*—why he is searching for you? "

"Well, what did he want? "

"Merely to tell you that your uncle, Mr. Eyre of Madeira, is dead, that he has left you all his property, and that you are now rich—merely that—nothing more."

"I! Rich? "

"Yes, quite an heiress."

There was silence.

CHAPTER 37

COUSINS

IT is a fine thing to be lifted in a moment from poverty to wealth, but not a matter that one can enjoy all at once. Besides, my uncle, my only relative, whom I had hoped one day to see, was dead.

"You raise your forehead at last," said Mr. Rivers. "Perhaps you will now ask how much you are worth? "

"How much am I worth? "

"Oh, a trifle! Nothing to speak of—twenty thousand pounds."

"Twenty thousand pounds! "

"Well," said Mr. St. John, laughing, a thing I had never known him do before, "if you had committed a murder, and I had told you your crime was discovered, you could scarcely look more upset."

"It is a large sum—don't you think there is a mistake? "

"No mistake at all."

Mr. Rivers now rose, and said good night. His hand was on the door, when a sudden thought occurred to me.

"Stop one minute! " I cried.

" Well? "

" It puzzles me to know why Mr. Briggs wrote to you about me, or how he knew you, or could imagine that you, living in such a lonely place as this, had the power to aid in my discovery."

" Oh! I am a priest, and priests are often asked for help about odd matters."

" No, that does not satisfy me! " I exclaimed, my curiosity aroused. " I must know more about this business."

" Another time."

" No, to-night! " and as he turned from the door, I placed myself between it and him. He looked rather embarrassed.

" I would rather Diana or Mary informed you."

My eagerness only increased, and I insisted once more on being satisfied.

" But I warn you I am a hard man," he said, " difficult to persuade."

" And I am a hard woman—impossible to deny."

" Well," he said, " I yield, if not to your eagerness, to your insistence. Besides, you must know some day—as well now as later. Your name is Jane Eyre? "

" Of course, that was all settled before."

" You are not aware, perhaps, that I am called St. John Eyre Rivers? "

" No, indeed! I remember now seeing the letter E in your name written in books you have lent me. But what then? Surely—— "

. I stopped. The truth rushed upon me, as circumstances began to connect themselves in my mind. St. John went on:

" My mother's name was Eyre; she had two brothers, one a priest who married Miss Jane Reed of Gateshead, the other, John Eyre, merchant of Madeira. Mr. Briggs, being Mr. Eyre's lawyer, wrote to us last August to inform us of our uncle's death, and to say that he had left his property to the orphan daughter of his brother the priest, giving nothing to us, as a result of a quarrel, never forgiven, between him and my father. He wrote again, a few weeks later, to say that the heiress was lost, and asking if we knew anything of her. A name written on a strip of paper has enabled me to find her. You know the rest."

"Do let me speak," I said, "your mother was my father's sister?"

"Yes."

"My Uncle John was your Uncle John? You, Diana, and Mary are my cousins?"

"We are cousins, yes."

I looked at him. This was wealth indeed, wealth to the heart.

"Oh, I am glad!" I exclaimed.

St. John smiled.

"Did I not say you neglected essential points in favour of trifles?" he asked. "You were serious when I told you you had got a fortune, and now, for a matter of no importance, you are excited."

"What can you mean? It may be of no importance to you; you have sisters and don't care about a cousin, but I had nobody, and now I have three relations. I say again, I am glad!"

I walked quickly to and fro. Thoughts rose more rapidly than I could express them. Mr. Rivers placed a chair behind me, and gently attempted to make me sit down.

"Write to Diana and Mary to-morrow," I said, "and tell them to come home directly. Diana said that a small sum of money would make a difference to them, so with five thousand pounds each they will do very well."

"Let me get you a glass of water," said St. John. "You must really try and calm yourself."

"Mr. Rivers! You make me lose patience. I am reasonable enough."

"Perhaps, if you explained yourself a little more fully——"

"Explain! What is there to explain? You must realize that twenty thousand pounds, divided equally among the four of us, will give five thousand each. I am not greedily selfish, blindly unjust, or wickedly ungrateful. This money could never all be mine in justice, though it might be by law."

"Jane, we will be your cousins, without expecting this sacrifice from you."

"Cousins—I, wealthy, and you, penniless!"

"And the school, Miss Eyre? It must now be shut up, I suppose?"

"No, I will keep my post of mistress till you get a substitute."

He smiled approval, and left me.

I had many struggles and used many arguments before I got the money settled as I wished. My task was a hard one, but as I was absolutely resolved on making a just division of the property, and my cousins must in their own hearts have felt that I was only doing what they themselves would have done in my place, they yielded at length so far as to allow the affair to be judged by lawyers. My opinion received support, the necessary papers were written out and signed, and St. John, Diana, Mary and I each became the possessors of a moderate fortune.

CHAPTER 38

MARY AND DIANA RETURN

IT was near Christmas by the time all was settled, and the holiday season approached. I now closed Morton School.

Mr. Rivers came. I saw the classes, now numbering sixty girls, pass out before me. I locked the door and stood with the key in my hand, exchanging a few words with half a dozen of my best pupils.

"Do you consider you have had your reward for a season of labour?" he asked, when they had gone. "Would not a life given up to the improvement of your race be well spent?"

"Yes," I said, "but I could not go on for ever so. I want to enjoy my own powers as well as to cultivate those of other people. I must enjoy them now: I am ready for a holiday. Don't remind me of school."

He looked serious.

"What is this? What are you going to do?"

"To be active. I want you to let Hannah help me. Diana and Mary will be home in a week, and I want to have everything in order for their arrival."

"I understand. I thought you were going off on some trip. Preparations in the house are all very well for the present, but I trust that later you will aim a little higher than domestic joys."

Hannah and I worked hard. When the house had been well cleaned, I bought new furniture and carpets and spent a good deal of time in arranging them.

The great day came at last. Hannah and I were dressed, and all was in readiness.

St. John arrived first. He found me in the kitchen, watching the progress of some cakes baking for tea. Approaching the fire, he asked whether I was at last satisfied with servant's work. He then went away to the sitting-room and began to read.

"They are coming! They are coming!" cried Hannah, throwing open the door. I ran out. The carriage had stopped at the gate. The driver opened the door: first one well-known form, then another, stepped out. They laughed, kissed me, then Hannah, and hastened into the house.

While the driver and Hannah brought in the luggage, they demanded St. John. At this moment he advanced from the sitting-room. They both threw their arms round his neck. He gave each one a quiet kiss, said in a low voice a few words of welcome, stood a short while to be talked to, and then returned to the sitting-room.

The evening was a happy one. My cousins were full of talk, and their conversation filled up their brother's silence. He was sincerely glad to see them, but he could not join in their gaiety.

The whole of the following week must have tested his

They laughed, and kissed me.

patience. It was Christmas week, and we were merry and unsettled. The freedom of home, the country air, and the dawn of prosperity, gave life to Diana and Mary, and they were gay from morning till noon, and from noon till night. St. John kept away from us; he was seldom in the house, but found daily business in visiting the sick and poor in Morton.

As our happiness grew calmer, we returned to our usual habits and regular studies. Mary drew, Diana read, and I worked at German. St. John, who now stayed at home more, studied some strange language which was necessary to his future plans. Thus busy, he appeared quiet and fully occupied enough, but his blue eye had a habit of leaving the curious-looking grammar, and wandering over and fixing upon me. I wondered what it meant. I wondered, too, at the constant satisfaction he showed at my weekly visit to Morton School. If the weather was unfavourable, and his sisters urged me not to go, he would always encourage me to do so. And when I returned, sometimes tired and wet from the rain, I never dared complain, because I saw that this would annoy him.

One afternoon, however, I was allowed to stay at home, on account of a cold. His sisters had gone in my place. I sat translating; he sat working at his grammar. I found myself under the influence of his ever-watchful eye. It searched me through and through, keenly and coldly.

" Jane, what are you doing? "

" Learning German."

" I want you to give up German and learn Hindustani."[1]

" You are not in earnest? "

" So much in earnest that I insist: and I will tell you why."

He then went on to explain that Hindustani was the language he was himself studying at present, in preparation for going to India as a missionary. As he advanced, he was liable to forget the beginning. It would help him greatly to have a pupil with whom he might again go over the first lessons, and fix them thoroughly in his mind. Would I do him this favour?

[1] Hindustani = the language of the Hindus.

I should not, perhaps, have to make the sacrifice for long, as he expected to be leaving in three months' time.

St. John was not a man to be easily refused: one felt that every impression made on him, either for pain or pleasure, was deep and permanent. I agreed.

I found him a very patient yet severe master. He expected me to do a great deal. Gradually he obtained a certain influence over me that took away my liberty of mind. I could no longer laugh or talk freely when he was near: I was fully aware that only serious thoughts and occupations were approved of. But I did not love my servitude, and I wished many a time that he had continued to neglect me.

CHAPTER 39

"JANE! JANE! JANE!"

NOT for a moment, amidst these changes of place and fortune, had I forgotten Mr. Rochester. The longing to know what had become of him followed me everywhere.

In the course of my letters to Mr. Briggs about the will, I inquired if he knew anything of Mr. Rochester's doings and state of health, but he was quite ignorant of all concerning him. I then wrote to Mrs. Fairfax, begging for information on the subject. I was astonished when two weeks passed without reply, but when two months went by and day after day the post brought nothing for me, I began to feel the keenest anxiety.

I wrote again: there was a chance that my first letter had been lost. Hope returned. Not a line, not a word reached me. When I had waited half a year in vain, my hope died out, and then I felt dark indeed.

A fine spring shone round me, which I could not enjoy. Summer approached. Diana tried to cheer me up. She said I looked ill, and wished to take me for a holiday by the sea. St. John opposed this: he said I did not want amusement, but

employment; my present life was too aimless.' He went on
still further with my lessons in Hindustani, and I, like a fool,
could not resist him.

One evening, I had come to my studies feeling sadder than
usual. Hannah had told me in the morning that the postman
had left something for me, and when I went down to take it,
almost certain that it was the longed-for news at last, I found
only an unimportant letter from Mr. Briggs on business. The
bitter disappointment had drawn some tears from me, and
now, as I sat struggling with the Indian writing, my eyes filled
again.

St. John called me to his side to read: in attempting to do
this my voice failed me. He and I were alone in the sitting-
room. My companion expressed no surprise at this emotion,
nor did he question me as to its cause. He only said:

"We will wait a few minutes, Jane, till you are more con-
trolled."

Wiping my eyes and murmuring something about not being
very well, I returned to my task and succeeded in completing
it. St. John put away my books and his, locked his desk,
and said:

"Jane, I want to have a talk with you."

He remained silent for some minutes, and then went on:

"Jane, I go in six weeks. I have reserved my passage on a
boat which sails on the twentieth of June."

I felt as if some fate was shaping itself for me. I trembled
to hear what he would say next. It came.

"Jane, come with me to India."

The room spun round me.

"Oh, St. John!" I cried, "have some mercy!"

He continued:

"God and Nature intended you for a missionary's wife.
You are formed for labour, not for love. A missionary's wife
you must, you shall be. You shall be mine. I claim you
for the service of God."

"I am not fit," I replied.

"I have an answer for you—hear it. I have watched you

ever since we first met. I have seen you pass several tests. In the village school I found you could perform, well and patiently, labour which was against your tastes and liking. By the calm with which you received the news that you had become rich, I saw that money had not too much influence over you. In the readiness with which you cut your fortune into four parts, and gave up three, I recognized that you had the power of self-sacrifice. In the obedience with which, at my wish, you gave up a study in which you were interested and adopted another because it interested me, I see a quality of the greatest use to my work. As a helper in Indian schools and among Indian women, your assistance will be of immense value to me."

"I should not live long in such a country."

"Ah! you are afraid of yourself," he said scornfully.

"What do you mean?"

"I know where your heart is. The feeling you are keeping alive is lawless and unholy. You think of Mr. Rochester."

It was true. I confessed it by silence.

The case was very plain before me. In leaving England, I should leave a loved but empty land. Wherever Mr. Rochester might be, he could be nothing to me. I must seek another interest in life to replace the one lost, and what occupation could be more glorious than that offered by St. John?

"I could decide if I were but certain," I said at last, "were I but convinced that it is God's will."

I sincerely longed to do what was right. "Show me, show me the right path!" I prayed to heaven. I was more excited than I had ever been.

All the house was still, for I believe all except St. John and myself had now gone to rest. The one candle was burnt out, the room was full of moonlight. My heart beat fast and thick, I heard its movement. Suddenly it stood still to an inexpressible feeling that ran through it. The feeling was not like an electric shock, but it was as sharp and as strange. It acted on my senses: eye and ear waited while the flesh trembled on my bones.

"What have you heard? What do you see?" asked St. John.

I saw nothing, but I heard a voice somewhere cry:

"Jane! Jane! Jane!"

It did not seem to be in the room, nor in the house, nor in the garden. It did not come out of the air, nor from under the earth, nor from overhead. I heard it, and it was the voice of a human being—a known, loved, well-remembered voice—that of Edward Rochester, and it spoke in pain, wildly and urgently.

"I am coming!" I cried. "Wait for me! Oh, I will come!"

I flew to the door and looked into the passage: it was dark. I ran out into the garden: it was empty.

"Where are you?" I exclaimed.

The distant hills echoed my cry, but all was lonely.

St. John had followed, but I asked him to leave me. He obeyed me at once. It was my turn to command. I went up to my room, locked myself in, and fell on my knees in prayer. I rose, my mind made up, and lay down, waiting for the daylight.

CHAPTER 40

BLACKENED RUIN

DAYLIGHT came. I rose and busied myself with arranging my things in order. I heard St. John leave his room, open the front door, and pass outside.

It was still two hours to breakfast-time. I spent the time in walking about my room, and reflecting on what had happened last night. I remembered that inward feeling that I had experienced, with all its indescribable strangeness. I remembered the voice I had heard; again I questioned from where it had come, as vainly as before: it had seemed *in* me—not in the external world. I asked myself if it was a mere nervous impression—a thing of the imagination. I could not believe it.

At breakfast I told Diana and Mary that I was going on a journey, and should be absent at least four days.

" Alone, Jane? " they asked.

" Yes, it is to see or hear news of a friend about whom I have for some time been anxious."

In their truly well-bred way, they put no further questions, except that Diana asked me if I was sure I was well enough to travel.

I left the house at three o'clock, and soon after four I stood at the foot of the signpost waiting for the arrival of the coach which was to take me to distant Thornfield. Amidst the silence of those lonely roads and hills, I heard it approach from far away. It was the same coach from which I had descended a year ago, in this very spot—how lonely and hopeless! Now, as I entered and was once more on the road to Thornfield, I felt like a homing pigeon returning.

It was a journey of thirty-six hours, and as the time drew on, the scenery with its green hedges and large fields and low hills, so much milder than the district from which I had just come, met my eye like the features of a familiar face.

" How far is it to Thornfield Hall from here? " I asked.

" Just two miles, ma'am, across the fields."

I got out of the coach, and left my box at the inn. The light shone on the signboard, and I read in gold letters, " The Rochester Arms." My heart leapt up: I was already on my master's lands: it fell again: the thought came to me:

" Your master may not be here, and even if he is, you can have nothing to do with him. You had better go no farther. Ask information from the people at the inn."

The suggestion was sensible, and yet I could not make myself accept it. I dreaded a reply that would crush me with despair. I wanted to look once more at the Hall. There was the stile before me, the fields, and the path. Almost before I had realized what I was doing, I was on the way. How fast I walked? How I looked forward to catch the first sight of the well-known woods!

At last they rose before me. I hastened on. Another field, a lane, and there were the courtyard walls and the buildings at the back. The house itself was still hidden.

"My first view shall be in front," I determined, "where I can see my master's window. Perhaps he will be standing at it—he rises early. Perhaps he is even now walking in the garden. Surely, in that case, I should not be so mad as to run to him?"

I had passed along the walls of the fruit garden, and turned the corner. There was a gate beyond, between two stone pillars. I advanced my head round one of them cautiously.

I looked with fearful joy towards a noble house. I saw a blackened ruin, with the silence of death about it.

CHAPTER 41

BLIND

I MUST have some answer to the questions that rushed through my mind. I could find it nowhere but at the inn, and there I returned.

The innkeeper himself brought the meal I ordered.

"You know Thornfield Hall, of course?" I managed to ask him at last.

"Yes, ma'am, I was the late[1] Mr. Rochester's butler," he replied.

"The late!" I exclaimed. "Is he dead?"

"I mean the father of the present gentleman, Mr. Edward."

I breathed again.

"Is Mr. Rochester living at the Hall now?"

"Oh, no, ma'am! Thornfield Hall was burnt down last autumn. A dreadful happening! Such an immense amount of valuable property destroyed. The fire broke out in the middle of the night. It was a terrible spectacle: I witnessed it myself."

[1] the late = the last, now dead.

In the middle of the night! That was ever the hour of fate at Thornfield.

" Do they know how it started? "

" They guessed, ma'am, they guessed. You are not perhaps aware," he continued, approaching a little closer, and speaking low, " that there was a lady—a—a madwoman, kept in the house? "

" I have heard something of it."

" This lady, ma'am," he went on, " was found to be Mr. Rochester's wife. The discovery was brought about in the strangest way. There was a young lady, a governess at the Hall, that Mr. Rochester was in——"

" But the fire," I suggested.

" I'm coming to that, ma'am—a governess that Mr. Rochester was in love with. The servants say they never saw anybody so much in love as he was. She was a little small thing, they say, almost like a child. Well, he was determined to marry her."

" You shall tell me this part of the story another time," I said, " but now I particularly wish to hear about the fire. Was it suspected that this madwoman was the cause of it? "

" It's quite certain, ma'am, that she started it. She had a woman to take care of her called Mrs. Poole, very trustworthy, except for one fault—she sometimes took a drink, and then her patient would steal her keys and escape. On this night the madwoman set fire first to the curtains in her own room, and then got down to a lower storey and burnt the bed in the room that had belonged to the governess, but it was empty, fortunately. The governess had run away two months before, and although Mr. Rochester sought her as if she were the most precious thing in the world, he could never hear a word of her; and he grew quite bitter with his disappointment. He wanted to be alone. He sent Mrs. Fairfax, his housekeeper, away to her friends at a distance. Miss Adele, a little girl who was in his charge, was put to school. He broke off all acquaintance with the neighbouring society, and shut himself up in the house."

" What! Did he not leave England? "

" Leave England! He would not move out of doors, except at night, when he walked like a ghost about the garden as if he had lost his senses—which it is my opinion he had; for I never saw a prouder, bolder, keener gentleman than he was before that governess upset him, ma'am. He was not so very handsome, but he had a courage and a will of his own."

" Then Mr. Rochester was at home when the fire broke out? "

" Yes, indeed he was. He went up to the top storey where all was burning, and got the servants out safely, and then went back to get his mad wife out of her room. They called out to him that she was on the roof, where she was standing, waving her arms and shouting. She was a big woman, with long black hair: we could see it blown against the flames as she stood. We saw him climb up to the roof. We heard him call, ' Bertha ! ' We saw him approach her, and then, ma'am, she screamed and leapt, and the next minute she lay motionless on the ground below."

" Dead? "

" Dead ! Yes, as dead as the stones on which her brains and blood lay scattered. It was frightful! "

" Were any other lives lost? "

" No—perhaps it would have been better if there had been."

" What do you mean? "

" Poor Mr. Edward ! Some say it was a just judgment on him for keeping his first marriage secret, and wanting to take on another wife while he had one living: but I pity him, my-self."

" You said he was alive? "

" Yes, he is alive; but many think he had better be dead."

" Why? How? " My blood was again running cold.

" He is blind."

I had dreaded worse. I had feared he was mad. I summoned up strength to ask the cause of his suffering.

" It was all his own courage and kindness. He wouldn't leave the house till everyone else was out before him. As he came down the great stairs, the roof fell in. He was taken out from under the ruins, alive, but badly hurt. One eye was knocked out, and one hand so crushed that Mr. Carter, the surgeon, had to take it off immediately. He lost the sight of the other eye as well."

"Where is he? Where does he live now?"

"At Ferndean, a country house on a farm which he owns, about thirty miles away."

"Who is with him?"

"Two old servants: he refused to have more. He is quite broken down, they say."

"Have you any sort of carriage?"

"We have a very handsome one, ma'am."

"Let it be got ready instantly, and if the driver can get me to Ferndean before dark this day, I'll pay both you and him twice the money you usually demand."

CHAPTER 42

"MAGIC IN THIS HOUR"

THE house of Ferndean was a building of moderate size, hidden deep in a wood. Mr. Rochester had often spoken of it, and had sometimes gone there. His father had bought the property for the sake of the shooting He would have let the house, but could find no one to rent it, because of its inconvenient and unhealthy position. It therefore remained uninhabited and unfurnished, except for two or three rooms fitted up for the use of the owner when he went there to shoot.

It was just before dark on an evening with dull sky, cold wind, and continual light rain. I dismissed the carriage and walked the last mile. Even when within a very short distance of the house I could see nothing of it, because the trees grew so thick and dark around it.

At last my way opened, and I stood in a space of enclosed ground before the house, scarcely visible in the dim light

There were no flowers, no garden, and all was still, save for the gentle fall of the rain.

"Can there be life here?" I asked myself.

Yes, there was life of some kind. I heard a movement: the narrow front door was opening.

It opened slowly: a figure came out into the twilight and stood on the step, a man without a hat, who stretched out his hand to feel whether it rained. Though it was dark, I recognized him—it was my master, Edward Rochester, and no other.

I checked my step, almost my breath, and stood to watch him—to examine him, myself unseen, and alas! invisible to him. It was a sudden meeting, and one in which joy was balanced by pain.

His form was the same strong one as ever, his walk still upright, his hair still black; nor were his features altered. But in his face I saw a change: he looked despairing, like some wronged and captive wild beast or bird, dangerous to approach in his sorrow.

He descended the one step, and advanced slowly towards the grass. Then he paused, as if he did not know which way to turn. He lifted his hand and opened his eyelids; gazed blank, and with difficulty, at the sky and towards the trees. I saw that to him all was empty darkness.

At this moment John, the servant, approached him.

"Will you take my arm, sir? There is a heavy shower coming on: had you not better go in?"

"Let me alone," was the answer.

John went in without having noticed me. Mr. Rochester, after vainly trying to walk about, felt his way back to the house and closed the door.

I now drew near and knocked. John's wife opened to me. She started as if she had seen a ghost.

I calmed her, and followed her into the kitchen, explaining in a few words that I had just heard what had happened since I left Thornfield. At this moment the bell in the sitting-room rang.

The servant filled a glass with water, and placed it on a tray, together with candles.

"Is that what he rang for?" I asked.

"Yes, he always has candles brought in at dark, though he is blind."

"Give me the tray: I will carry it in."

I took it from her hand: it shook as I held it. The water spilt from the glass; my heart beat loud and fast. John's wife opened the door, and shut it behind me.

The sitting-room looked gloomy. A small, neglected fire burnt low in the fireplace, and leaning over it was the blind owner of the room. His old dog, Pilot, lay on one side, but jumped up and ran to me, almost knocking the tray from my hands. I set it on the table, and said softly, "Lie down!" Mr. Rochester turned to see what the disturbance was, but remembering his weakness, moved his head back again.

"Give me the water," he said.

I approached him. Pilot followed me, still excited.

"What is the matter?" he inquired.

"Down, Pilot!" I said again. He checked the water on the way to his lips, and seemed to listen. He drank and put the glass down.

"Who is this? Who is this?" he demanded. "Answer me—speak again!"

"Pilot knows me, and John and his wife. I have just come," I answered.

He put out his hand with a quick movement. Not seeing where I stood, he did not touch me; I put my hand in his.

"Her fingers!" he cried. "Is it Jane? This is her shape —this is her size——"

"And this her voice," I added. "She is all here: her heart too. God bless you, sir! I am glad to be so near you again."

"You are real? You are altogether a human being, Jane? You are certain of that?"

"I conscientiously believe so, Mr. Rochester."

"Yet how, on this dark evening, could you rise so suddenly in my lonely room? I stretched out my hand to take a glass

The servant filled a glass with water, and placed it on a

I put my hand in his. (Page 153)

of water from a servant, and it was given me by you: I asked a question, and your voice spoke in my ear."

" Because I came in with the tray in place of John's wife."

" There is magic in this hour. Who can tell what a dark, hopeless life I have dragged on for months past? Doing nothing, expecting nothing, conscious only of an unending sorrow, and at times a mad desire to see my Jane again. How can it be that Jane is with me? Will she not depart as suddenly as she came? "

I was sure that a practical reply was best for him in this state of mind. I asked him when he had his supper.

" I never have supper."

" But you shall have some to-night. I am hungry: so are you, I expect—only you forget."

Summoning John's wife, I soon had a meal on the table. I was excited, and I talked to him during supper and for a long time after with pleasure and ease. There was no feeling of restraint, no holding back of life and laughter with him. With him I was happy, because I knew I suited him. It brought light to my whole nature. Though he was blind, smiles began to dawn on his face, and his features lost their look of bitterness.

" Whom have you been with all this time, Jane? "

" You shall not find that out from me to-night, sir. You must wait till to-morrow. Now I'll leave you. I have been travelling these last three days, and I believe I am tired. Good night."

" Just one word, Jane. Were there only ladies in the house where you have been? "

I laughed and went away. Here I saw the means of rousing him out of his gloomy thoughts.

CHAPTER 43

WHOM I LOVE BEST

VERY early the next morning I heard him go downstairs. As soon as the servants came down, I heard the question, " Is Miss Eyre here? " Then: " Which room did you put her in? Is she up? Go and ask her if she wants anything, and when she will come down."

Entering the breakfast-room very softly, I had a view of him before he discovered my presence. He sat in his chair, lines of sadness marking his strong features.

" It is a bright, sunny morning, sir," I said. " The rain is over and gone. You must go for a walk."

I had roused him to life. He smiled.

Most of the morning was spent out of doors. After a time he urged me to tell of my experiences during the last year. I began my story, but I softened the description of my three days of wandering a good deal.

He told me that I should not have left him thus, without means of supporting myself. He was certain I had suffered more than I had confessed to him.

" Well, whatever my sufferings were, they were short," I answered. I then told of my welcome by the Rivers family, and of all that followed.

" This St. John, then, is your cousin? "

" Yes."

" You have spoken of him often: do you like him? "

" He is a very good man, sir; I could not help liking him."

" A good man. Does that mean a respectable man of fifty? "

" St. John is only twenty-nine, sir."

" Is he a short person, dull and plain? "

" He is a handsome man: tall, fair, with blue eyes."

" But his brain? It is probably rather soft? "

" He talks little, sir, but what he says is always worth listening to. He is a truly intelligent man."

" Did you like him, Jane? "

" Yes, Mr. Rochester, I liked him: but you asked me that before."

Jealousy had got hold of him, but the sting was bringing him back to life.

" Did he visit you often at your school? "

" Daily."

" You had a cottage near the school, you say: did he ever come there to see you? "

" Sometimes."

A pause.

" Did Rivers spend much time with the ladies of the family while you were living with them? "

" Yes, we worked in the same room."

" What did you study? "

" I learnt German, at first."

" Did he teach you? "

" He does not understand German. He taught me a little Hindustani."

" Rivers taught you Hindustani? "

" Yes, sir."

" And his sisters also? "

" No, only me."

" Did you ask to learn? "

" No, he wished to teach me."

" Why did he wish it? Of what use could Hindustani be to you? "

" He intended me to go to India with him."

" He wanted to marry you? "

" He asked me to marry him."

" That is an invention, to annoy me."

" I beg your pardon, sir. He did ask me, and was as earnest in urging me as ever you could be."

" Miss Eyre, you can leave me. Go and marry this Rivers."

" He will never be my husband. He does not love me, nor I him. He wanted me only because he thought I should make a suitable missionary's wife. He is good and great, but too cold for me. Must I leave you, sir, to go to him? "

" What, Jane! Is such really the state of affairs? "

" Absolutely, sir."

" You wish to be friends, Jane? "

" Yes, sir."

" Ah, Jane, but I want a wife."

" Do you, sir? "

" Yes: is it news to you? "

" Choose then, sir—her who loves you best."

" I will at least choose—her whom I love best. Jane, will you marry me? "

" Yes, sir."

" A poor blind man, whom you will have to lead about by the hand? "

" Most truly, sir."

A little later, he said:

" Jane, a curious thing happened to me a few days ago. I think it was last Monday night. I had long had the impression that, since I could not find you, you must be dead. Late that night I began to pray for death also. My punishment, I felt, had lasted long enough: I asked God to end it. My heart's wishes broke from my lips in the words—' Jane! Jane! Jane! '

" You will think I imagined things, but what I tell you now is true. As I called, a voice, I cannot tell from where, replied: ' I am coming: wait for me,' and a moment later the words— ' Where are you? ' were whispered on the wind. In spirit, I believe, we must have met."

CHAPTER 44

THE END

I MARRIED Mr. Rochester very quietly a few days later. I wrote immediately to my cousins to say what I had done. Diana and Mary approved the step without hesitation. How

St. John received the news, I do not know. He never answered the letter that I sent him on the subject. Six months later he wrote to me calmly and kindly, but without mentioning Mr. Rochester's name. He has since written regularly, though not frequently, from India, where he is giving his life to his work.

I soon went to see little Adele at her school. Her wild joy at seeing me again filled me with pity. She looked pale and thin. I found the rules of the school too severe for a child of her age, and I took her home with me till I could find a more suitable establishment. When she left school, I found her a pleasing and grateful companion.

Mr. Rochester continued blind for the first two years of our marriage. Then, one morning, as I was writing a letter at his dictation, he said:

" Jane, have you a glittering ornament round your neck? "

I was wearing a gold chain. I answered: " Yes."

" And have you a pale blue dress on? "

I had. He then informed me that he had fancied for some time that the darkness clouding one eye was becoming lighter, and that now he was sure of it.

He and I went up to London. He had the advice of a famous eye specialist, and in time recovered the sight of one eye. He cannot see very distinctly, but when his son was put into his arms, he could see that the boy had inherited his own eyes as they once were, large, bright and black.

Diana and Mary Rivers are both married, and come to see us every year. Diana's husband is a captain in the navy, Mary's a priest, a college friend of her brother's. Both are happy.

St. John is unmarried. He will never marry now. The last letter I received from him showed only too clearly that his work on this earth is nearly over. He has no fear of death, and the end will come to him as he has wished.

LONGMANS' SIMPLIFIED ENGLISH SERIES

GENERAL EDITOR : C. KINGSLEY WILLIAMS, M.A.

PRIDE AND PREJUDICE*
Jane Austen

THE CORAL ISLAND
THE GORILLA HUNTERS
R. M. Ballantyne

THE JACARANDA TREE
H. E. Bates

SIX SHORT PLAYS
edited by J. A. Bright

JANE EYRE
Charlotte Brontë

WUTHERING HEIGHTS
Emily Brontë

PRESTER JOHN
THE POWER HOUSE
THE THIRTY-NINE STEPS
John Buchan

THE GOOD EARTH
Pearl S. Buck

THE MOONSTONE
THE WOMAN IN WHITE
Wilkie Collins

HATTER'S CASTLE
THE CITADEL
A. J. Cronin

A TALE OF TWO CITIES
Charles Dickens

IN THE SERVICE OF THE QUEEN
THE THREE MUSKETEERS
A. Dumas

ADAM BEDE
George Eliot

CRANFORD
Elizabeth Gaskell

MONTEZUMA'S DAUGHTER
Sir H. Rider Haggard

A WONDER BOOK
Nathaniel Hawthorne

PIONEERS OF PROGRESS
C. S. S. Higham

THE PRISONER OF ZENDA
RUPERT OF HENTZAU
Anthony Hope

CAMPBELL'S KINGDOM
Hammond Innes

THREE MEN IN A BOAT*
THREE MEN ON THE BUMMEL
Jerome K. Jerome

TALES FROM SHAKESPEARE

MORE TALES FROM SHAKESPEARE
Charles & Mary Lamb

FRENCHMAN'S CREEK
JAMAICA INN
REBECCA*
Daphne du Maurier

MOBY DICK
Herman Melville

BARLASCH OF THE GUARD
H. Seton Merriman

TALES OF MYSTERY AND
    IMAGINATION
Edgar Allan Poe

SHAKA ZULU
E. A. Ritter

THE UNPLEASANTNESS AT
    BELLONA CLUB
Dorothy Sayers

THE TALISMAN
Sir Walter Scott

DR. JEKYLL AND MR. HYDE
KIDNAPPED
R. L. Stevenson

VANITY FAIR
W. M. Thackeray

A BOOK OF SHORTER STORIES
BRITISH AND AMERICAN SHORT
    STORIES
OUTSTANDING SHORT STORIES
edited by G. C. Thornley

THE THREE CLERKS
Anthony Trollope

THE ADVENTURES OF HUCKLE-
    BERRY FINN
THE ADVENTURES OF TOM SAWYER
Mark Twain

A JOURNEY TO THE CENTRE OF
    THE EARTH
ROUND THE WORLD IN EIGHTY
    DAYS
Jules Verne

THE INVISIBLE MAN
H. G. Wells

A GENTLEMAN OF FRANCE
Stanley Weyman

THE WOODEN HORSE
Eric Williams

THE KRAKEN WAKES
John Wyndham

* *also issued in a hard cased binding*